Day of the Not-So-Dead
And Other Morbid Little Holiday Tales

Day of the
Not-So-Dead

and
Other Morbid Little Holiday Tales

Robin Martinez Rice

RLMR

ISBN: 0692782591

ISBN-13: 978-0692782590

ACKNOWLEDGMENTS

Buckets full of thanks to Marlene Koons for all her beta reads, rush jobs, helping me learn how to pass things back and forth digitally and so much more. I am only half a writer without her. And thanks to my editor, Laura Buckner for jumping on the wagon with a rush job and realizing there is no point in talking to me about comma placement or sentence fragments.

You noticed. Not all the stories are holiday tales. And yep, you got it again. They aren't all so morbid. Although they might be if you stop and think about it.

There is a social test within these stories. There should be one story that rubs you the wrong way, seems odd, or some such thing. Email me the title of the story and why it bothers you and I'll let you in on the secret.

robin@robinmartinezrice.com

CONTENTS

DAY OF THE NOT-SO-DEAD

Maria Conseula Rodriques y Dominguez was tired of looking at the old photographs. What had started as a quick chore had gone on for days. She never realized how many boxes of photos her mother had tucked away in closets, not to mention the garage and the tool shed.

Her mother had died six months ago and this year it was up to Maria to get the altar ready for *El Día de los Muertos*. Family tradition and all. But the thing was, Maria didn't believe in ghosts. Shouldn't each generation be allowed to start their own traditions?

Her sister Rosie didn't agree. "Family is important, Maria. I already told the kids about the celebration. I would help, you know I would. But Joe has a soccer tournament and I have to make Halloween costumes for all four kids this year."

Under the words Maria couldn't help but hear her sister's thoughts—"and you don't have any kids." Rose, the good daughter, who quickly popped out four grandchildren in ten years for Mama to enjoy before she got sick.

1

Was it a crime to forego marriage and children? Maria secretly thought she looked a lot better than her sister. At thirty-two she could pass for twenty-five. All those kids? Rosie looked forty.

Maria closed the box and wiped dust from her hands. That was the last of it and there were no pictures of Daddy. She tried to remember the altars Mama had constructed on the mantel each year, then realized she had never paid much attention to the details. Had celebrating the dead ever included Maria's father?

Maria was six years old the last time she saw Francisco Pedro Contesso Dominguez. Better known as Frank. For years she thought she remembered exactly what her father looked like, how he tossed her in the air when she ran to wrap her arms around his legs—when he showed up—how he tickled her neck just under her ear with his fuzzy mustached kisses, how he tucked her in each night with a story and a strange lopsided hug. He only used one arm to squeeze her and the other always held a cigarette. But when she went away to college she had watched an old movie on late night television and the scene from her memory was there. In the movie. And the actor named Hernando Garcia who had hugged the child actress and tossed her in the air, was a replica of her mental picture of Daddy. Maria realized she didn't remember her father at all. The visions and the images —they had all been wrong.

"Did I ever see the movie *Busque Los Ángeles*?" Maria had asked her mother when she visited.

"Of course. Many times. That was your grandmother's

favorite." Mama looked up from the pot of stew she was stirring. "I hated it. I was so tired of her watching it again and again. But you liked to watch with her, so I let it pass."

Her mother looked into the pot, then walked to the refrigerator. "He was always the hero to her, never the villain. No matter what he did, he could still win her heart."

Her grandmother was in love with an actor? That didn't sound like Granny. She was level headed. Hernando Garcia must have made other films, not the one Maria remembered where he played a loving father. Maybe there were movies where he was the bad guy. She would have to look them up on the internet.

"Did Daddy have a mustache?" Maria knew her mother didn't like questions about Frank.

"Hmmm...when he was young he did. But it gave him a rash, so he shaved it off."

Maria had to accept that the fuzzy mustached kisses in her mind were from Hernando Garcia, and that the actor had never really kissed her neck, just the little girl in the movie. And she couldn't help but wonder, had Francisco Pedro Contesso Dominguez ever tucked her in at night?

She called her sister. "I can't find any pictures of Daddy," she said, twisting the cord around her finger. They could probably sell this old rotary phone on e-bay, a real collectors item.

"She got rid of them." Rosie sounded distracted.

"Do you have any?"

"Me? Why would I have any? He left us, Maria. Don't you

remember how terrible it was?"

Maria didn't want Rosie to know that she didn't remember. None of it. That in her mind her father was a not-so-well-known actor, not a man whose face she couldn't recall. "What about his favorite food? I can put that out if I don't have a picture." Even if she didn't believe in ghosts, she wanted Daddy in the altar.

"He liked those gooey orange candies. But why are you including him at all? Stick to Mama, Granny and Pop Pop. If you're feeling sentimental, put out some dog bones for Chickita. Mom always included her in the altar." Clearly Rosie had studied Mama's displays more than Maria ever had.

So Mama included the vicious Chihuahua mutt in the celebration of the dead, but not Daddy. Did the dog really deserve her favorite treats while Frank, ex-husband and ex-father, didn't get any recognition? Just the thought of Chickita made Maria's finger throb and she looked at the thin white scar which connected her knuckle with her fingernail—a memento of the precious pet. Was she wrong to wish for a memento of her father?

Maybe if Rosie came over she would find something amid all this junk that had belonged to their father. "We need to clean out the house," Maria suggested.

"I know, Maria. I told you I can do it in December. It's waited this long, it can wait a few more weeks."

A few more weeks? It was October. But Maria kept her mouth shut. No use inflaming her sister. That fire burned too hot already.

The usual crowd of men was gathered in front of the labor exchange. He would be old, too old to be among the men waiting for work, but she couldn't keep herself from studying the faces. She looked for Daddy here every time she walked to the store. Just as she looked for him in old blue pickup trucks because she remembered what his truck looked like, even if she couldn't recall his face. For twenty-six years she had searched for her father. She couldn't stop now.

When Maria got home from the market she took the candy bar, the red and white packet of cigarettes and the tiny bottle of Jim Beam out of the sack and set them on the mantel in front of the photos she had placed there.

She rubbed a finger across this picture of Mama. The smooth skin, the shiny long hair—her mother must have been about sixteen. Had she met Frank yet? Slept with him? Not pregnant though. Rosie was born when Mama was twenty-two. Late for a woman in this town to have a first baby. An old maid, Mama had joked. But when Maria asked about her father—Was it love at first sight? What was your first kiss like?—Mama had refused to say more than "I was very young when we met. Too young and he went away. Then he came back."

He went away. He did it to Mama many times, but he came back. And then he did it to me, Maria thought. He came back to Mama but he never came back to me.

Did he have a new family? Was there someone else propping a photograph on the mantel to celebrate The Day of the Dead? Was a different daughter placing tabasco sauce and orange wedge candies out for the ghost of her father to enjoy? Did she have something else of his to add—a tie, a belt buckle, a pipe? Things that this better daughter could touch and smell and remember, while Maria had nothing. Just a false memory.

She propped the postcard of the Virgin next to Mama. She had tried to find a picture of Santa Librada, the saint her mother swore got rid of headaches, but she seemed to be a somewhat obscure virtuous being. Maria was happy when Rosie inherited Mama's migraines, and she escaped without the terrible pain that attacked her mother and her sister at least once a month.

Maria was healthy. She never broke a bone, even though she fell out of the cottonwood down by the creek. She never had colds or the flu and she had the Certificate of Perfect Attendance to show for it. Did she take after her father?

After she put Pop Pop's and Granny's pictures on the altar, adding a cigar she had found in the kitchen drawer to the candy, whiskey and cigarettes, she called Rosie.

"What time do you want to go to the cemetery on Saturday?"

"Joe has basketball, then Mark has piano, I pick up Mitzy at three, how about five-thirty?"

"At night?" The sun set by six this time of year. Did Rosie want to traipse her kids through the graveyard in the dark? "I thought we would go in the morning. You know, take the flowers early so they are there all day."

"I can't. You go ahead. I'll see them when we come."

Maria put the heavy receiver back in its cradle.

She drove to Pasqual's Nursery to look for flowers. There were none in the yard this time of year and truth be told she had neglected Mama's garden. Angry that she had to move back to the house. Angry that Rosie's logic was sound—Maria didn't have a job or a home and Rosie did, therefore Maria was the one who should move back. Angry, angry, angry.

As she picked through the faded blooms, she tried once again to remember her father. The memories had to be in her head somewhere. She was six when he left, not a baby. Maybe she should try hypnosis.

Had he loved her at all? She knew how Mama could be when wronged. Stubborn and resentful. Full of the knowledge that mothers always knew best. Maybe Mama forbid him from seeing them, kept him away. Maybe she had tossed away the birthday cards and Christmas presents he sent to his daughters.

Her sister had to remember him. Rosie was eight when he left. Why wouldn't she tell Maria about him? Was there more to the secret?

It wouldn't be the first time her sister kept the truth from her. Rosie hadn't called to tell her about Mama's cancer until it was too late. Maria hadn't been there to go to the doctor appointments, to listen to the information and convince Mama she did need the chemotherapy, the radiation, the treatments. To convince Mama to live.

"It was her decision, Maria." Her sister had puffed up with importance, acting as if she had said or done nothing when Mama decided it was time to die. Maria knew there was no way Rosie had kept quiet about it. If she had, it was the first time in her life her sister had kept her opinion to herself.

Maria decided to go to the cemetery on Thursday. It would be crowded on Friday, the day to honor the dead children, and Saturday would be a crazy mess. Whenever *El Día de los Muertos* fell on the weekend, scores of relatives celebrated. Thursday was Halloween and people would be focused on trick-or-treating and parties for the kids.

There was one other car in the parking lot, a beat up Ford Focus that had definitely seen better days. Maria spotted a figure three graves away from Mama's resting place. The man, who was very tall and wearing an old-fashioned felt hat, stood with bowed head. She looked away. She wanted to respect the lone mourner. And she needed him to give her space.

A few plastic flowers decorated some of the graves but no one had arrived yet to put food and pictures and belongings out for the dead to celebrate. By Saturday these small rectangles of honor would be covered with color—flowers, piñatas, food, and belongings would dress up the drab gray and brown landscape of *Montaña Dormida* Cemetery.

Maria sat down on a stone next to the grave—no grassy knoll in New Mexico, just the yellow sand and dry dirt—and leaned the jar of dahlias against the small headstone.

Rosa Maria Rebekah Rodriquez, born March 12, 1957. Died April 7, 2013. Blessed are the sinners who repent for they shall not be alone.

Which sinners had her mother thought about when she asked that this be carved upon the stone? Her AWOL husband? Herself? Did Mama hope to be with Frank after she died?

Maria fell to her knees and pushed her hand against the dirt which covered the grave.

"Mama. Who was my father? I need to know him. Why didn't you tell me about him when you knew you were leaving me?"

She didn't feel anything. No sense of her mother's spirit, no soul, no ghosts floating around the cemetery. Her mother was dead. There would be no use for the things Maria had brought to help her mother's spirit get through the night: the sewing basket with its thread and needle, the sweet *biscochitos*, or the bottle of diet cola Mama loved. She would set them here, in the dust, on the lonesome grave, the dirt covering the body with no one in it. Mama wasn't here. Maria would leave the things but only for Rosie's children to enjoy. Her mother was long past the time of pleasure.

Maria heard mumbling and she turned to look at her fellow mourner.

The man at the other grave was old. He had removed his hat and held it clutched in front of him. His hair was thin and his suit wrinkled. Surely he was the driver of the sad Ford Escort. He noticed her looking at him, grinned and then shrugged.

It was the shrug that did it. Maria gasped and stared at the man. Those eyes, still dark behind the broken red veins. That mustache, the fuzzy caterpillar she remembered. And that shrug, she would know it anywhere.

"Hernando Garcia?" She choked out the words in a hoarse whisper.

The old man smiled and walked toward her. When he stood next to her he reached out a hand. "At your service, my dear. Let me help you up."

"You live here?" She took his hand and he pulled her up from the dirt.

"Just visiting." He laughed and waved toward the grave down the row. "My wife."

"I'm sorry. I didn't mean here. I meant in Albuquerque." Maria blushed. "You must get tired of people interfering with your private life."

"I am never bothered by a fan. And I am flattered to be recognized by one so young. It has been many years since I made a film."

Maria watched as Hernando patted his pockets, then removed a cellophane package. He reached across his body and tapped the pack on his elbow to remove a thin brown cigarette. He slipped the package back into his pocket and pulled out a square box of penny matches.

Marie was mesmerized. She traveled back in time as she watched. She had seen this before. She knew what would come next.

Hernando used only one hand to slide the box open and flip out a single match. Pinched between his thumb and finger he struck it on the side of the box.

Maria watched him light the cigarette stuck between his lips and draw in a deep breath. He let the smoke out slowly, so that a cloud formed around his face.

"I...you...," she stuttered. For a moment she had been so sure the memory was real, that this man was her father and not just some mixed up hope.

He hadn't recognized her. If he was Daddy, he would have known her.

Maria felt the old sense of abandonment crash down on her with the force of a baseball bat. A sharp pain shot through her head, just above her right eye and she covered it, pressing at the lightning bolt which pierced her brain. She slumped back to the rock. "Santa Librada help me," she whispered. Was this what her sister went through with those headaches?

Maria spoke without uncovering her face. "I'm sorry. I am mistaken. I just thought…"

She heard the crunch of his footsteps move past her and she pulled her hands away from her eyes. The old man was looking at Mama's headstone.

He turned to her. "Are you Maria or Rosie? You inherited her headaches, I see. I didn't know Rosa had died. I would have been here."

Two days later, with the sun setting and the cemetery taking on an eerie feeling, Maria stood next to Rosie as the kids placed gifts upon Mama's grave.

"I found him. I remembered him. All that time, I thought I was wrong, thinking about Hernando Garcia. But I wasn't. He was an actor. He was Hernando Garcia."

"Mark, don't push your sister." Rosie shifted the baby to her other hip. "Found who? What actor?"

"Daddy."

Her sister looked around at the scattered graves and then turned to face her. "Here?"

"No. Well, yes. But not buried." Maria took a deep breath. "Alive. He was visiting his wife's grave."

"Mama's grave?"

"No. Not Mama. His wife, Grace Carson."

"What are you talking about?" Rosie turned away and took a step toward her children, shaking her head. "Mark, one more time and you're waiting in the car."

Why couldn't Rosie focus on what she was saying for just one minute? "He was married to someone else. He had another family. After he left us."

"You talked to him? He…you…he told you about this other family?" Rosie finally turned and faced her. "Wait a minute. You need to start at the beginning. I'm finding this really hard to believe."

But just then Maria caught sight of her ghost. He parked his old car and walked through the dim light. She saw how stooped he was, how the old hat was ripped on one side, how his suit sagged at the elbows. She pulled the bag of orange wedge candy from her purse.

"If you don't believe me, you can ask him yourself." Then she turned and walked toward her father, imagining how it would feel when he wrapped one arm around her and squeezed, holding his cigarette away from her face so that she didn't have to breathe his smoke.

HAUNTS BE GONE

All the ghost stories I ever hear'd, those haunts were angry. They hung around for revenge, or to expose their killer or to finish some undone work. And it weren't never pleasant.

So when that doctor lady or therapist or whatever it was she called herself told me that maybe I needed to listen to what Mindy was saying to me, I knowed she was way off base.

Not-even-in-the-outfield off base.

"Mr. Brown, can you close your eyes and take a deep breath?"

I closed my eyes.

A split hair of a second later I opened them.

"Are you'all trying to use that hypnotism on me? Cause if you are, I'm a tellin' you, it ain't gonna work."

My eyes were open long enough to see Mindy poke her head out from behind the curtain. Her face was red and angry and her lips were moving a mile a minute. But I still couldn't make out her words.

I slammed my eyes shut and dove under the scratchy

hospital sheet.

"Mr. Brown. There is no need to be frightened of me. I am not hypnotizing you, just trying to get you to relax. It would help if you took the blankets off your face."

Next thing I know I'm a shakin' and a screamin' a'cause Mindy made her way right under those sheets. She sat on my chest and pressed, then covered my mouth with her smooth, pink hand. Far off I hear'd the therapist lady call for help and someone come into the room and they shot something into that tube in my arm and finally Mindy ran out and I could breathe again and then I slept.

I musta slept for a long while, 'cause when I woke up the sun was gone. Night time is different in a hospital. All quiet like, which is good if you're sick and need some rest but not so great if you are trying to get away from the ghost of the woman you killed.

No don't go jumpin' to any dark conclusions. I didn't murder her, but I killed her just the same and far as I can tell she don't see the difference. Maybe if things hadn't gone south between us last year she would be more understandin' and I wouldn't be hiding under these blankets every time she pokes her head through that door, or out from under the bed, or from behind the curtains or just walks in with that cat-who-ate-the-canary smile on her face and sits there in that chair reserved for bedside visitors.

It all started when we were but kids, she was fourteen and I was sixteen. I'd a habit of doing what every sixteen year old boy in love does. I'd follow behind her when she walked home from school and throw rocks her way.

"Henry Brown, if one of those rocks hits me you better run for all you're worth," she'd call out.

I wasn't worried. I had a sharp arm and good aim. Warn't no way one of those rocks would hit her. But they'd come close enough to give her a thrill and that gave me a thrill, hearin' her voice sing-song with make-believe anger.

Warn't long before we were walkin' together and not long after that I held her sweet hand. I held it at the movies, I held it at church, and finally after three years I held it down the aisle at Marktown Baptist and we moved into that old shed out behind my Uncle Clay's barn.

Mindy loved that old shed. She sewed up curtains and a quilt for the bed and I painted and sanded and nailed boards where boards needed to be nailed. It was as fine a home as any young couple could want.

Only thing is, it wasn't as fine a home as any not-so-young couple could want. I planned on living there 'til I died. Warn't any job other than working as Uncle Clay's right-hand man that I needed. He was the most patient man ever lived. Taught me how to fix a truck, how to plow a field, how to cure a cow of all that ails her.

"You need to find a job that pays," Mindy decided.

When I shrugged and took a swig of beer, why she didn't argue. Just went on out and got herself a job of her own.

"Those new houses out at Diggers Corners have a low down payment. If you brought in five hundred dollars a month, we could buy one." She tapped her fingers on the scratched wood of the kitchen table. Nice oak table I found out at the dumps. Only needed a little work.

"He's taking advantage of you," she nagged.

I stepped out to the barn and dug out the bottle of hootch tucked behind that old tractor that none of us could repair. The twang from the beer wasn't enough to drown out her words.

"What are we gonna do when he dies?" She wouldn't let up.

"He ain't sick. Why you want to say something so cruel?"

But Mindy, she was smart and she had the eye. The one that can see into the future. 'Cause sure enough, Uncle Clay died within the year. And Mister Darthmo, who it ended up actually owned that farm, he didn't see fit to keep me on and before you knew it the whole place was all plowed under and a big new Walmart stood where my wife's yellow curtains had sparkled in the morning sunlight, and that floor I had sanded on my hands and knees and tenderly buffed to a high shine was only so much landfill.

So things went south. Way south. Mindy worked harder and I drank harder. We moved into a trashy apartment 'cause I couldn't find no single person at all to pay me that five hundred dollars a month. Plus, those houses were all sold by then and there weren't no other place for folks like us. So when I brought home that old blue Chevy, she wasn't too pleased.

"Where'd you get the money for that piece of crap?"

"Helped Drake move some wood." Truth was I wanted to surprise her with some extra cash, but Drake couldn't pay me and the old truck of his seemed like a fair trade. With the

automotive skills Uncle Clay had taught me, I knew I could get her near good as new.

"Let's go for a drive, Min. It'll feel good. We can have us a picnic to celebrate Independence Day."

"What do you want to celebrate independence from? Maybe I'll leave you and go to Grantville and get me a better job and a better house." She had been talking to her sister again. That girl wanted Mindy to come live with her and tried to convince her she'd be better off without me.

" Ahh, come on Min. We'll have fun. We can be free up there in them hills. Wind'll blow our troubles away." Being as the truck didn't have a passenger window, you couldn't really escape the breeze.

She caved. "Fine. I'll go so you'll quit your whining."

Her little snub nose wrinkled from the minit she got into that truck. And it warn't two seconds after the naggin' started.

"Slow down, Henry. I can't catch my breath with all this wind." Mindy pulled her scarf down and tried to tie it under her chin.

"Ah...chill out a little." I stepped on the gas and the old tires squealed around the corner.

"I mean it. Slow down." She slammed her hand on the dash. "Better yet, stop this old heap and let me out. I've lost my desire for a picnic."

Lost her desire for me, that's really what she was sayin'.

I planned on slowin' down. I didn't want to scare her. I really did want to have a nice day with my wife. I reached over and pulled a beer from the bag on the floor.

"Do you have to drink that now?"

I popped the top, and took a drag. "I wouldn't if you'd quit harpin' at me."

Then that old truck, as if it were on her side, jerked to the left and the steering wheel whipped out of my hand. I grabbed and pulled hard to turn her back, but she didn't want to do what I was askin' and leaped off the road.

After the truck quit rolling down the hill, bangin' and a screamin' all the way, it stopped top-side-down. Mindy was under me and we were pressed together something awful as some part of the crashin' and rollin' had sunk that old roof down tight.

I could hear whimpers but when I tried to move there wasn't even an inch of space.

"Get off, I can't breathe, get off me."

I felt Mindy twitch and I tried to shift to one side to give her some air. She was makin' a sound like my old granny what died of the lung ailment. Mindy's face was down by my stomach and try as I might I couldn't give her no air. I pressed up as hard as I could, thinkin' about that super-human strength that comes over folks in a tight situation, but I didn't seem to have it and the metal vice I was locked in didn't give, not even enough to let a trickle of air into her lungs. I cried and cried, but then I was worried with her under me like that what if my tears were drownin' her on top of my big old beer belly, keeping her lungs from pulling in air?

It wasn't long before she quit movin'.

It was an eternity before someone came and cut me out of

that coffin.

So Miss Therapist, you see, I don't really want to hear what Mindy is trying to tell me. I'm pretty damn sure it ain't "I forgive you, Henry." So if you don't mind, give me a bit more of that sleeping juice into that tube and I'll just keep my eyes closed tight. And if you all want to stay here while I sleep, why that'd be fine, 'cause maybe with you as my watchdog Mindy'll stay back there in the corner and keep away from sittin' on my chest again. Maybe I can keep suckin' oxygen into my lungs for one more day.

'Cept I miss her sumtin' fierce, so maybe I'll just let her come up here into this bed with me. And maybe I'll beg her to let me breathe, or maybe I won't.

Have Yourself a Debt Free Christmas

Dorothy reached into her purse. As soon as she grasped the worn plastic wallet she knew she was in trouble.

Damn Slade. He had robbed her of all her cash again.

"Just a sec," she told the gum-chewing clerk. The expression on the young woman's face was blank—she didn't care what happened—but Dorothy was very aware of the long line of holiday shoppers waiting behind her.

She opened her wallet. Three dollars. That bastard hadn't even left her enough for lunch. She tapped her finger on the credit card tucked behind her driver's license, then looked at the bags hanging on the twirly bagging rack.

She and Slade had agreed that once the credit cards were paid down they would use them for emergencies only. Since Dorothy was laid off last year she had spent all her time job hunting but other than a two hour gig as a lunch lady at the elementary school, nothing had come up. Cash was tight for the Nelson family right now.

The bags held presents for the kids and Slade, shampoo and toothpaste, and some knit gloves for her. Cheap, but a wonderful purple color she couldn't resist. She had lost one of her gloves last week and the weather was turning.

"Hey, what's the problem up there?" The crazed shoppers behind her were impatient.

"How much did you say it was?" Dorothy looked down at the little keypad, but her eyes were filling with tears and she couldn't read the numbers.

"One hundred eleven and fifty-two cents."

"Come on lady—shit or get off the pot."

Dorothy couldn't believe how crude these people were. Biting her lip, she swiped her card.

On the drive home she pounded the steering wheel with her palm. How would she hide the charges from Slade? He would come unglued when he discovered that she had used the card only six days after their decision. They couldn't be in debt again, couldn't survive it. Not only the money, but the stress.

Maybe Christmas was an emergency. Surely Slade would agree that the kids shouldn't go without presents?

It wasn't until Dorothy was home, unpacking the two bags— not much for over a hundred dollars—that she realized Slade was to blame. When she left to go shopping she had cash in her wallet, at least she thought she did. He was the one who had robbed her of her promise not to use that credit card. She would confront—no, discuss—it with him tonight, weeks before the bill came. The last thing she needed to do was let him find out she was hiding something from him. It would be another weapon in

22

his arsenal for their constant fights.

"Slade—"

"Can you believe it? That red light on the dash again. I'll have to take the car in tomorrow before work. What's for dinner?"

Damn. This meant he would be using her car. It was also the kind of thing that *was* an emergency and the cost of the repairs would go on the credit card.

"Casserole. The chicken tortilla thing."

"Well, let's eat. I'm going to try a few things on the car tonight and maybe I can fix it."

As far as Dorothy knew, Slade had never fixed a car in his life.

She waited until he gulped down half the food on his plate before she tried again. "I was surprised that there was no money in my wallet today."

"I told you last night I needed cash today."

Dorothy bit her tongue. She didn't want a fight.

Slade didn't fix his car and he did take hers the next morning. He promised to be home early—James had tutoring. One more essential item that they couldn't afford, but failing Algebra was out of the question now that it was a graduation requirement. Dorothy had failed Algebra, which gave her added sympathy for her son's predicament.

She looked at the clock for the twentieth time. Slade was cutting it close. Finally she heard the car pull into the driveway.

"Come on James. Dad's home and we need to get moving."

Slade pounded on the door. It was just like him to refuse to use his key and expect her to be a doorman as well as cook and chauffeur. When she let him in, he pushed his way past her and plopped a huge silver urn onto the dining room table.

"Slade! Careful, you'll scratch the table. What is that?"

"A samovar. Like a vase or something. Mom had it up in her attic. It's an antique. I remember it from the summer I spent in San Francisco with Babushka and Dedushka. They kept it on their mantel."

Vase was not the word Dorothy would have used to describe this object. It was like an overgrown tea pot, with two handles on the sides, just like that children's song. She touched the edge and the black crust flaked off. Must not be real silver.

"Needs some polish." She tried to be supportive. It seemed obvious that this pot meant a lot to Slade.

"Don't mess with it, Dot. I want to have it appraised and try for that television show. If you clean it that cuts into the value."

Value? Was there something special about this thing? If Slade wanted to sell it, maybe it wasn't such a sentimental object.

"Come on Mom. You're the one that said we were going to be late." James stood at the door, his algebra book in hand.

She got back from the tutoring session to find the pot perched on the mantel with a framed photo of Slade's grandparents next to it. Esfir and Abram didn't seem impressed. Their stoic expressions felt accusatory—as if Dorothy herself had somehow forced them to leave Russia. Her grandmother's brass candlesticks had been relegated to the end table. She could already see a brown ring under the samovar. Of course Slade hadn't bothered to put a cloth of any type underneath the tarnished base.

He muted his television program long enough to ask about dinner. As Dorothy was headed to the kitchen the phone rang.

She pulled lettuce and hamburger from the refrigerator and listened to Slade.

"Uh huh. Hmmm…so replacement, not repair. Jeez. Sure… okay…no choice, really….That long?"

He set the phone down and came into the kitchen.

"It's the fuel injectors. Completely shot."

"How much?"

"Three hundred."

Dorothy cringed. Slade's car was only five years old. Their newer car. But not under warranty because they had bought it used, as is.

"It won't be done until Saturday. I'll need your car tomorrow."

Dorothy shrugged. There wasn't anywhere she had to be. Her lunch hour job was within walking distance. At least Slade still had his job. Even so, he had a moratorium on overtime that pushed them closer to insolvency every day.

Dorothy sighed as she rinsed the dishcloth and draped it over the detergent bottle to dry. Another day had passed and she hadn't told Slade about the credit card. Tomorrow would be too late. He would assume she'd kept the new charges hidden on purpose.

She had.

"So this...pot—"

"Samovar." Slade buttered his toast and watched the morning news, not glancing away from the television as he corrected her.

"I looked it up. I don't think it is a samovar. Those were like coffee pot things, for heating water. They have a lid and a spigot. I can show you a picture online."

"Show me."

Slade studied the photos, scrolling down and then clicking on to the next page of her web search. "Here." He clicked a photo to enlarge it. "It *is* like this one."

Slade's pot was similar to the picture, but no lid or spigot. Just like she had told him.

"It belonged to your grandparents?"

"Older than that. I think my grandfather's grandfather. It's probably hundreds of years old."

"Well most of these seem like from they're the 1800s. A big price range, though." Dorothy studied the offerings. Here was one for $2000, but right next to it was one for $49.95.

She pushed the morning newspaper across the table and tapped an advertisement in the lower right hand corner. "They're coming to town."

Slade sopped up his runny egg with the last of his toast and pushed his glasses up his nose. "I'd love to find out what it's worth. I heard the show can be a scam, though."

"How so?"

"Tell you something is worth three times what you can really get for it. They have to make it exciting for the viewers."

"Maybe we should just have it appraised. There are people who do that kind of thing."

Dorothy had gone online and checked the credit card balance. Over $500 now. They wouldn't be able to pay the whole thing off this month. The interest would snowball just like it had last year.

"Appraisers charge a fee. If they're in town, sounds like my destiny. I'll try out for that show. Can't hurt." Slade ripped the ad out of the paper and stuffed it in his shirt pocket as he left for work.

"Hey Dot. I can't get the damn password to work. Did you change it?" Slade tapped the return key rapidly as he spoke. As if knocking on a door when he knew someone was home but they were refusing to let him in.

"Which password?" Dorothy knew which account he was having trouble with. She had changed the credit card password last night.

"The Visa. I need to check the balance. I want to make sure that slimy garage deducted my deposit."

"Are you sure you capitalized the "G"? It's case sensitive, you know."

"Crap. Now I'm locked out."

"Easy, Slade. It's for our protection. I'll call them tomorrow and figure it out."

As he shut down the computer Dorothy walked out to the garage with the trash. One day to figure out how to keep him from seeing the balance on the card. She stuffed the bag into the trash bin and leaned against the car. Her gaze fell on the boxes of linens she had moved when Dad died last year. Pillow cases, table clothes, collars never sewn onto dresses—all decorated with detailed needlework. Her mother had been a nervous woman and the close focus of her embroidery had calmed her. Dorothy couldn't remember an evening when Mom hadn't had a hoop and needle in her lap.

She missed her parents. Everyone knew that Dad wouldn't last long once Mom died. Dorothy had felt like an orphan when she packed up their house. A reverse mortgage had seen them through their last years but it meant her inheritance was in these boxes, stacked in the garage, of no value to anyone. The linens, mismatched Fiestaware, odd assortments of cartoon glasses that fast food joints had given away in the 1970s. Slade complained that two cars wouldn't fit in the garage with all the stuff, so Dorothy kept her car outside now.

If only he would go on that show and the silly urn was worth a bunch of money. Twenty thousand would do it. She had seen it happen. Even ten thousand would see them through the winter. In spring she would find work. Landscapers would need some help and she had a real green thumb.

Dorothy got home from the market on Saturday afternoon and discovered Slade had covered the kitchen table with newspapers. He was brushing the black crumbling grime from the samovar.

"Look! It does have a lid." He held up a silver hat. "I asked Mom about it and she found it."

"It's shiny."

He snorted. "She polished it. Now I can't decide if I should polish the whole thing or just take it like this."

"When do you go for the show?"

"Tuesday. You aren't really filmed. You stand in a long line and then they tell you if you come back for the filming or not."

Tuesday was only three days from now. Three short days if you are waiting for a chance at a television show. Three long forevers if you are trying to find money to pay your debts.

"I'm not likely to sell it, you know that right? It belonged to my ancestors."

"Then why are you doing all this?"

He laughed. "Curiosity, nothing more. Gotta know how much this thing is worth."

Slade decided to polish the samovar. He spent the evening listening to one of his right-wing radio talk shows and rubbing away. When he finished he set the shiny silver pot back on the mantel, lid in place. He went up to bed, leaving a mass of rags and newspapers scattered around the kitchen.

The article caught her eye, just as she crinkled the stained paper. Extended Holiday Hours at the permanent flea market on the edge of town. Usually it was only opened on weekends, but apparently Christmas was a good season there as well. It could work. If she sold some of the linens and dishes stored in the garage she would have some cash for Christmas. There really wasn't any need to hang on to that stuff.

And maybe, just maybe, it would give her a little leverage in convincing Slade to sell the samovar.

On Monday the flea market was a success. They were happy to let her set up her card table, although she was in the back corner of the parking lot. It didn't matter because folks were serious in their searches for valuable items. They went to every table and scanned, made quick offers and packed their shopping bags full of treasures. She sold all of the linens she had brought and kicked herself for not bringing everything. She hadn't wanted to haul it all down if she couldn't sell it. Now she knew the cartoon glasses were practically made of gold, particularly if she had some complete sets. And quilters loved embroidered linens.

She did a little shopping of her own. A barely used machine for video games and some roller skates. A nice leather belt for Slade. And she still had enough money to cover the things she had put on the credit card.

Any day now he would remember that he needed access to the statement. She would talk to him tonight.

"Hey Dorothy. Will you look at this?" Slade was on the computer as soon as the last morsel of dinner had been gulped down by her hungry family. She had a rule about no television during the meal, but all that accomplished was kids who ate fast and rushed off. All those articles about family night and meaningful conversations didn't exist in this tribe.

Slade had found a full page of samovars. She looked over his shoulder at one that appeared to be identical to Babushka's pot—arms akimbo but no spigot.

"Five thousand smackaroos! Not too shabby for an old pot."

"Slade," Dorothy paused.

He didn't turn away from the screen, but at least he answered. "What?"

"The credit card balance, it's over $500."

Now she had his attention.

"Damn it. So that slimy bastard didn't credit my deposit. I knew it." He slammed his fist on the table.

"No. It's just, that day you borrowed my cash. Remember? I had to do some shopping and I put it on the card."

He had turned back to the screen and was scrolling through the samovars again. She really only had half his attention.

"I thought we agreed emergencies only."

"You're not being fair, Slade. You took my cash. I thought I had enough."

"I told you I was taking it. You should have checked."

"But the samovar? It can take care of all of this. Don't you see? It would tide us over until I get another job."

"You want me to sell my inheritance, the one and only thing I have from my grandparents? To pay for your shopping spree?"

"It wasn't my shopping spree. It was toothpaste and dish soap and toilet paper. I'm not the only one in this house who uses those things."

"What about all that crap in the garage? Why don't you sell that?"

"I did."

Slade stopped scrolling. "You sold that stuff? Where's the money?"

"I used it for Christmas presents."

"Oh, I see. You use your inheritance for what you want, but mine has to bail us out of your mess."

Dorothy closed her eyes and took a deep breath. She considered counting to ten as a backup plan, while she repeated her mantra: *don't say it, don't say it, don't say it.* It won't do any good to tell him he is being so unfair.

"It's just a thought, Slade."

"Yeah? Well this is one of those times you should keep your damn thoughts to yourself."

She told herself he wasn't really mad at her. He had suffered this year too. It wasn't easy for a man to feel he couldn't provide for his family.

On Tuesday the kids had dentist appointments so she couldn't go with Slade to the audition. Not that he had invited her.

Dorothy was surprised that he was already home when they got back. Not a good sign. Wouldn't it take longer if he had been picked for the show?

"I'm in! They liked the fact that this thing has been in my family. Made me list all the Russian ancestors I could remember. Even coached me on talking with a bit more of an accent."

"When?"

"Tomorrow. They only stay in town for two days. Today for

interviews, tomorrow for shooting the show."

"What time do we have to be there?" She would wear her blue silk dress. Long sleeves so the wrinkles and folds on her arms were hidden from the cameras.

"You weren't there today, what makes you think you would go tomorrow?" Slade shook his head. "I need to call Mom. She's going to be over the moon about this."

It turned out the show wasn't broadcast live. It wouldn't air for months. Dorothy stayed home and watched TV anyway. What else was there for her to do?

At one o'clock she decided to bake. It would be nice to have cookies for Christmas, just a few days away. And she didn't want Slade to guess that she was sitting around waiting for him to return.

He burst through the door without the samovar. "What a day, what a day!"

"You sold it?"

"What?" He shook his head as he finally processed her question. "No. It's in the car."

"So?"

"Let me get something to drink, will you? It's been a long day."

A long day? It was only one thirty.

"Would you like a slice of pie?" The cookies hadn't been all she baked. "Just took it out of the oven."

"Sure, sure." He pulled various bottles out of the cupboard and set them on the counter. "Where's that vodka Uncle Sam gave us?"

"I don't know, dear. How about some coffee instead?"

"So now you think I drink too much? Is that what you're saying?"

"Of course not. I'm just thinking about what goes nice with pie." Actually she just wanted him to tell her about the samovar. "So how much is it worth?"

Slade shrugged. "The whole thing was a joke, really. Some expert. He didn't know anything about Russia. Kept dropping phrases about Moscow, as if that's the only city in the biggest country on the planet."

"So what did he say?"

"Two thousand dollars. Not in good shape. Spigot missing and some other fiddle-faddle about no adornments."

"Two thousand? That's quite a bit, Slade."

"Stop right there. I'm not selling it. I made that clear, didn't I? Ahh...here it is." Slade found the vodka and grabbed a glass. He poured a generous serving and left everything on the counter. "I'll be watching the news. You can bring my pie in to me."

As Dorothy cut the pie—it was too hot, the filling still runny —she thought about the linens and the Fiestaware still in the garage. She would use them. She would replace their bargain sheets and pillow cases with the nice things her mother embroidered and display the colorful dishes on the shelves. She would be reminded of her mother every day, but in a good way. She had happy memories of eating off those dishes. That was her inheritance. She had planned on taking the rest of the stuff to the flea market tomorrow, and she would. She would take her dad's tools and those cartoon glasses, but not her mother's things.

Slade grabbed the pie from her and turned his attention back to his program. "Hey, I'm bushed. Will you go out and bring the samovar in? It's not heavy. Just prop the door." He was watching some sort of junk collector show. His new thing.

The samovar *was* sort of heavy, and very awkward. She tried to lift it by the handles, but it tipped forward and the top fell off. One more thing for Slade to get on her case for. She wiped it off with her apron and examined it, rubbing the tip of her finger over a small dent. Had that been there before? With a sigh she tucked the lid inside her pocket, then heaved up the pot.

When she made her way into the house she could see that Slade had finished his pie and set the plate on the floor by his chair. The chair was empty because he was in the kitchen pouring more vodka. She set the samovar on the table.

"That's not where it goes." Slade made his way back to his recliner and flopped down with a grunt.

Dorothy rubbed her hands on her apron and looked at the back of her husband's head. There was fat around his neck, visible because he kept his hair razor short. When they met he had long curls touching his collar. His hair was a shiny blond and his eyes so blue. He had been a total gentleman, courting her in every sense of the word.

But now. Now she was standing next to a relic that could buy some relief. But he was too selfish.

He owed her. She might be out of work right now but she had worked hard all those years. And kept up the house. And taken care of the kids. He never lifted a finger around here.

Never changed a diaper, never went to an orthodontist appointment, or never stayed up late to help finish a science project.

Dorothy picked up the samovar with every intention of putting it on the mantel. Before she could set it back on the stained spot Slade had left, an odd sensation took over—the top of her head was light, as if she might faint. Her vision clouded as she lifted the urn high over her head and brought it down on Slade's skull. There was an odd ringing crunch and he slumped over without a sound.

Instantly she awoke from her shock. "Slade, Slade. I didn't mean—" She waved her hands near him, but didn't touch him. Was he breathing?

Thank goodness the kids weren't home. She grabbed the samovar and raced out to the car. If she got rid of it and called the police as soon as she got home, it would look like a home invasion.

She drove down the street, thinking that she would head to the dump. But those guys would remember her, wouldn't they? A woman getting rid of a single item, and one that didn't look like trash at all? She turned toward the Salvation Army store. A donation, that's what she would do.

Two blocks later she passed the gate to the flea market. Folks were setting up for tomorrow—Christmas Eve. The biggest shopping day of the year. Dorothy made a sharp right and pulled into the vendor gate.

She grabbed the last two tens from her wallet and paid the attendant.

"Space 83. Second row on the left. All vehicles out by five o'clock."

At Space 83 she pulled out the card table. It was a good thing she had already loaded the car for tomorrow's sale. She spread a large table cloth so that the edges hung nearly to the ground. She arranged her father's tools on it, then slipped the samovar underneath, so it was hidden.

She moved her car to the parking lot and waited. It was only three-thirty and she had to wait until there were fewer people around.

What if Slade wasn't dead? She would have to convince him he was attacked while she wasn't home. On television the victim never accurately remembered the assault. It was nearly five and most people were leaving. They had covered their tables with tarps and sheets, apparently not concerned about theft.

She walked quickly back to her space. Just across the aisle was a double booth filled with all kinds of metal stuff. Mostly old farm equipment, but there was a tea pot and a table filled with dishes. Dorothy looked around once more, then carried the samovar across the aisle. She set it on the ground next to the table, but it looked out of place. She lifted a stack of cake plates and stacked them on the dinner plates. She moved a milk pitcher over to the table with the tools. The samovar looked right at home on the table, and she could only hope that more than one person manned a booth this big and that they would all think someone else had brought the urn to sell.

It wasn't until Dorothy was driving home, mentally preparing her phone call to the police, that she felt the weight of the samovar lid in her pocket. She pulled over and slumped against the steering wheel. This couldn't be happening. She hadn't really killed her husband, had she? She should have checked his pulse. He was probably just knocked out and when she got home he would be boiling mad.

She pulled to a stop next to a vacant lot beside the same damn mega store that had started this whole fiasco. She was never going to shop there again. Taking the lid from her pocket, she wiped it off with the table cloth. Then she rolled down the window and threw it, watching it spin into the tall yellow grass.

"Say so long to your inheritance, Slade."

ROSE COLOR GLASSES

Charlene felt a pinch of guilt which started in her stomach and slowly inched up into her chest. When she reached the stop sign and gave a slight nod to the dusty hitchhiker, her heart was tight and her breath was shallow. He stood on the edge of Crosstown Boulevard, at eight fifteen every day. Maybe he had to arrive at work at eight thirty, just like she did.

He toted a backpack, so he must be homeless. Could homeless people have jobs? Wasn't there some rule about an address and a paycheck? Charlene had watched a program about it once; she recalled the catch-twenty-two aspect of the homeless ever making progress back to a better life.

She fought the urge that hit her every morning. She wanted to pull over and give him a ride. *Remember that woman in Utah. Or the girl in Oregon. Bodies found or, worse yet, bodies never found.* It was too risky to help him. She turned her head and accelerated, keeping her eyes on the road. By the time she pulled into her parking space—her name in block letters on the concrete tire stop—her breathing was perfectly normal.

Day after day she saw the man until she no longer noticed him. He had become as routine as the new stop sign at the corner of Gully and Main or the purple house on Fifth Street. Your attention might be drawn magnetically the first time you saw these oddities, but the image was soon filed into some deep recess of your neurons. She nodded if he caught her eye, but more often her mind was ticking rapidly through her list for the day: *look up the Bargood account, remind Theresa to pull the numbers for the first quarter and figure out the bottom line on why they had doubled the number of copies, stop for toilet paper and dish soap on the way home.*

On Friday when the horrendous bang caused her to scream, and the thumping that followed told her this was a blown out tire and not a gunshot, she pulled to the side of the road without thinking about the man.

"Damn it." She kicked the tire and looked at her watch.

"Can I help you with that?"

The voice came out of nowhere and Charlene screamed again.

"Sorry, I didn't mean to scare you." He set his tattered pack on the ground and reached out a hand. "I'm Todd. I can change that for you."

She stepped back, her hand going to the door handle. To her embarrassment she tucked the other hand in her pocket, as if he might grab it and force her to shake.

He backed away, the scowl on his face one of someone not used to being repulsive.

"Sorry. I...I'll leave."

As he turned Charlene thought about bad things happening. But not to her.

To him.

His eyes were a sparkling blue and his shaggy hair showed signs of having been cut at some point in time. His clothes were clean, although one boot had a knotted yellow and black striped lace and the other a red string holding it closed. He wore a silver watch attached to a leather band and a tiny gold stud in his right ear.

Terrible things must have happened to get him to this place. And he was trying, wasn't he? With the job and all? Then she remembered that she didn't really know if he had a job—she had imagined that part.

"No. Please. I'm sorry." She took a step toward him. "I was just scared by the noise of the tire. It made me—" What did it make her? More of a bitch? A snob? Scared of him? "I'm Charlene. It would be great if you could help. I can pay you."

She didn't reach out a hand, but she returned his smile.

Todd changed the tire with such ease, Charlene decided he must be a mechanic. She wanted to make small talk, to ask him where he worked, how he became homeless, if he was hungry, but the words stuck in her throat. What if he turned and hit her with that long part of the jack? She strolled over to the side of the road and pretended to study the wild flowers while she took a twenty dollar bill from her wallet, hiding the rest of her cash in the bottom of her purse.

Todd wouldn't take the money.

"Don't worry about it. Glad to help." He smiled and picked up his pack. "I could use a ride into town."

Charlene shook her head hard. "I...I'm not going to town. I remembered something else." She quickly jumped in the car and closed the door. "But thanks, thanks so much," she called through the closed window as she slipped her rose colored sunglasses back on her nose and stepped on the accelerator a little too hard, gravel spinning from beneath her newly changed tire as she sped away.

BETTER

The first thing Ben noticed when he moved from 4th Avenue to 181st SE was Manuel's Coffee House on the corner. He could walk to his new job and stop for morning coffee, all within two blocks of the apartment. Sure, it was on the third floor, not the point of living in a luxury high rise, but the thought of no more waking in the predawn blackness, no more two hour drives, no more wasted hours spent in his tiny car on the jammed bridge, memorizing the pigeon nests and rust spots day after day—these things pleased him. Even no more car, because the Fiat was on the final gasp of its combusting life cycle. An oil change or tune up couldn't squeeze any more miles out of the junker so Ben got rid of the car.

The first morning in his new home was just as he had imagined. He woke before the alarm—set for eight o'clock rather than five-thirty—the sun was shining and he had time to check out the coffee choices offered at the tiny, non-chain, close to home, coffee house.

The aroma of roasting beans was thick enough to taste. The

floors were scuffed linoleum, the old style he remembered from his grandmother's kitchen. Probably clean, but so worn their gray color made the place look rather dowdy. There were no chairs or tables in the shop. A long counter stood in the center of the room, awkwardly bisecting the small space with its shining espresso machine—a Gaggia no less. A cash register and an old mayonnaise jar adorned with a handwritten "tips" message crowded what little space was left. The barista who greeted him with a grunt and a stare was grizzled, the gray of his scruffy beard the same color as the floor. His once-white apron was splattered with something quite unappetizing, greens and browns blending together in an abstract blur.

Ben had second thoughts about the place.

"What'll it be?"

A whiteboard was propped against the wall. Coffee 3, Espresso 4/ 4^{50}, Mocha 4/4^{25}, Latte 3^{75}/4, Cappuccino 4^{50}/5.

"Uh, just a coffee."

A scowl and a paper cup were accompanied by a wave to the corner. Apparently Manuel was not into customer service. Ben took the cup and handed over a five dollar bill. The old man punched several keys on the register, resulting in a tinny "bing," the clatter of the drawer springing open, and the receipt spitting out like a sassy tongue. He ripped it free and pulled a pencil stub from his pocket. Ben watched as the barista circled the total then turned over the slip and drew what seemed to be a circle on the back. He plucked two bills from the drawer, slapped the receipt on top and handed the bundle to Ben.

Ben glanced at the tip jar, then slipped the change into the pocket of his wool coat. He never tipped out of habit, his father had seen to that. Everyone must earn their rewards, just or not. The tip would come after he tasted the coffee.

A black and silver machine perched like a vulture on a narrow shelf tucked in the back corner. Ben hadn't seen one of these ancients in person, but he recognized it from the classic movies he watched when his insomnia drove him to flip through late night TV. Two silver brewing baskets below, and a warming burner on top—no pump thermos in this shop. The old style glass coffee pot wore a sheen of mud colored residue. The liquid inside was as dark as tar.

"Thanks," he managed to squeeze out between tight lips. He filled the cup, took a lid from the precarious stack on the edge of the counter and left.

The sun warmed the cold city and the wide sidewalk, and the smiling doormen in front of each luxury apartment drove the grimy feel of the shop from Ben's mind. He sipped the coffee cautiously.

It was good.

He sipped again.

Better than good. This had to be the best coffee he had ever tasted. Even the aroma was different. He sipped and sniffed and sauntered to work. No rushing on this fine morning.

Margaret, according to the placard on her desk, greeted him with a perfect smile, white teeth shining nearly as much as the silver sign welcoming him to Meyers and Browning.

"You must be Mr. Grigg. Let me show you to your office." She rose. Perfect body too.

Ben followed her down the long hall.

"Henry would like to see you at eleven fifteen. Do you know where his office is?" Without waiting for him to answer Margaret continued. "I'll come by and take you up. This place is a maze."

"Thanks." He had only been here once, for his interview. A different version of Margaret, older but no less beautiful, had led him up and down the halls on that day.

It was all Ben could do to keep from gushing and losing his manly posture when Margaret led him through the door of an office. His office. Desk twice the size of his last job, floor to ceiling windows with a view of the bridge. The very same bridge he had been stuck on for the last two years.

"Will this work for you?"

"You bet." Ben didn't try to keep his school-boy excitement at bay.

"Let me know if you need anything." Margaret flashed those teeth once more and left him to gloat over the spoils.

The sun never quit shining on Ben that day. The stack of folders on his desk held leads to clients, which took advantage of his real skills—negotiation and presentations—unlike the slave labor at Parsons Inc. Henry Browning proved to be a boss who treated him like an adult—the eleven fifteen meeting had included a trip out to lunch at the city's finest steak house—and the ever-helpful Margaret was icing on the cake.

Ben walked home as the golden orb of sun settled atop the skyline, whispering goodnight after a perfect day. He glanced at the coffee house, the front covered by a rolled down security grate, and for a moment he could swear the smooth smell of this morning's coffee wafted through the air and walked home beside him.

On Tuesday there were two people in line. Manuel wore a green apron today, no cleaner than the other. This one looked like it had been used as a paint rag—reds, yellows, and blacks created an abstract worthy of display in an alternative gallery.

Ben studied the whiteboard while he waited. Maybe he would try an espresso today, although yesterday's coffee had been great.

"What'll it be?"

"Is the four-fifty espresso a double?" Ben didn't want to pay extra if the difference wasn't significant. The move, the new job, the new clothes for the new job—cash flow would be an issue until his first pay check.

"One size." Manuel shook his head and pointed to the stack of paper cups.

An impatient voice snarled. "Come on buddy, we don't have all day."

He hadn't noticed that there was a line of people behind him.

"Espresso, the single," he pulled out his wallet.

"The four dollar?"

"Right." He pulled four bills from his wallet.

"Four-fifty is better."

"Two shots?"

Manuel shook his head and held up his index finger. "It's better."

This was crazy. "No, just the four." Was this some sort of

plan to get a tip? If people had change they were more likely to toss it into the old jar. Ben wasn't going to fall for that old trick.

"I don't need the receipt." Ben waved his hand as Manuel pulled out his pencil. The guy behind him was still chomping at the bit.

The barista shook his head, circled the total and drew what Ben now supposed was a happy face on the back. Ben snatched it from the counter and stuffed it in his pocket, feeling the crumple of yesterday's receipt. What a waste of paper.

The espresso was good, but nothing like the delicacy of yesterday's coffee.

Ben stopped at Manuel's every day. He didn't try any of the other drinks, already addicted to the coffee. Then one day, two weeks into his new job and still happy as a seagull with a discarded bologna sandwich, things changed.

"Good morning," he said, smiling at Manuel, although the old man never returned the greeting. "Coffee."

The barista shook his head. "Not today."

"What?" Ben smiled again. Ah...the guy had a sense of humor after all.

"She's broken." Manuel pointed at the whiteboard. "You pick something else."

Ben looked over at the coffee pot. Sure enough, it was unplugged and no grimy glass pot sat below the aluminum brewing basket.

He was disappointed. The coffee was part of his morning ritual. He used the time to sip and think during the ten short minutes he spent walking to the silver skyscraper.

"You like espresso?"

The espresso had been okay, but nothing like the coffee. Ben shook his head.

"Maybe cappuccino?" Manuel tapped his thick fingers on the counter.

"Okay." Four-fifty? It better be good. "I'll take the small one."

"One size."

Back here again. Ben looked over his shoulder. He was the only one in the shop today, which was unusual. "What's the difference then? Between four-fifty and five?"

"The five, she's better."

"Better? Do you mean an extra shot?"

"No."

If it wasn't bigger and it didn't have an extra shot what was different? Ben glanced at his watch. This was taking too long. He would have to rush to make it to work on time.

"No. The four-fifty will do."

The cappuccino was good, certainly better than many he had tried, but it did not fill the need he had for Manuel's coffee.

The lack of coffee seemed to be a cosmic sign that Ben was due for a bad day. He was late, in spite of walking quickly through the sidewalk throngs. Stepping through the huge doors of Meyers and Browning, he glanced toward Margaret's desk only to see a different woman seated in her chair. No butterfly, the replacement was a drab moth. A moth who didn't smile.

"Where's Margaret?"

The moth shrugged. "I'm just a temp."

The temp secretary did not know where to find the files Ben needed. In fact, it seemed all she knew how to do was answer the phone with a bland "Meyers and Browning," then put callers on hold while she wandered around trying to find someone who could answer whatever inquiry had come over the line. The third time she interrupted him with her lame questions, he snapped.

"I am not a secretary. Quit bothering me."

Even a moth can look angry and hurt.

Walking home, two hours later than usual, Ben was drawn to the coffee house. He stopped and tried to look at the coffee machine through the window. The shop was dark and the security grate kept him from pressing his face close enough to see through the unwashed windows. Had the old clunker been repaired?

To top off the day—what was that children's book? The terrible-no-good-day?—when Ben called Anna to see if she wanted to meet him for dinner this week, she blew him off.

"I'll call you."

Had she really said that? To him? When he was on such a roll? Why would Anna break up with him now of all times? She had stuck with him through the last years of college, the crazy low paying intern jobs, the hovel he had lived in.

"Did I do something wrong?"

"No, no. I'm just busy this week. You know how it is. I'll call you, I promise."

Ben knew her right cheek would be twitching. Anna's tell—especially when she was stressed or lying. There was something in her voice that didn't reassure him.

Ben scowled at the sight of the coffee machine huddled quiet and dark on its shelf. He wasn't overly impressed with the espresso or the cappuccino, so today he would try the mocha. He handed Manuel four dollars. "Mocha, please."

"You have a quarter?"

"I just want the small one."

"Only one size. Four twenty-five."

The old barista folded his left arm across his chest and held out his right.

"Okay," Ben searched his pocket. He set a quarter into Manuel's outstretched palm. "What's the difference?'

"It's better."

The mocha was good, delicious, in fact. As Ben had never had Manuel's chocolate before, he didn't know if it was better than the four dollar version, but it was every bit as good as the coffee he craved.

"Morning, Mr. Grigg." His day was improving, Margaret was back.

At eleven o'clock Anna called. "I have a cancellation. Can you catch lunch with me?"

He wondered if she had decided to break up in person. "Sure."

She didn't. Wasn't. Had no intention of breaking up with him. Over pasta and salad she told him about the new client she had signed and her face glowed with confidence. She hadn't wanted to commit to anything this week because she needed to keep her schedule free until she knew she had won the contract. He knew Anna was superstitious, which was probably why she hadn't told him all of this last night.

The next day the coffee pot blinked its red light and a very clean and shiny glass pot sat under the drip. Ben was about to order his usual coffee when the whiteboard caught his eye. There was a new entry.

Mexican Latte 6/6^{75}.

He was curious enough to pull out the bills and three quarters.

"I'll have the Mexican Latte."

Manuel nodded and turned to the Gaggia.

Ben watched the old man pour the beans into a grinder, press the lid with a growl that matched that of the machine, scoop the mixture into the silver cup, and latch it into place. He slopped what looked like muddy river water from a glass jug into the cup.

Ben took a cautious sip. Images of Aztec queens filled his mind and his tongue burned, not in a hot way, but with a spicy tingle. He took another swig and swore he heard the call of a parrot.

"What's in this?"

"It *is* better." The corner of the old man's lip edged up ever so slightly and Ben almost imagined there was going to be a smile, but the barista didn't go that far.

"Thanks. It's great." The exotic drink entertained Ben all the way to work. He was disappointed when he finished it and for a moment considered turning back for another. Silly, he thought. You need to get to work.

Later that day Ben had a visit from Mr. Meyers. The company was happy with his work. They were going to skip the usual six months probationary period and offer him a permanent contract now.

Happy *Cinco de Mayo* to me, Ben thought, suddenly realizing why Manuel was offering the Mexican Latte today.

For six months Ben stopped in and pulled out his cash, always adding the quarters now for the "better" version of Manuel's drinks. Coffee was his standard fare, but he came to love the other choices too. And Manuel's occasional special drinks were not to be passed up; each one a more exotic blend of aroma and taste. He was used to Manuel's eccentricities—the grunts for replies, the daily insistence on the choices, the barely perceptible nod when a coin was slipped into the tip jar. And those crazy receipts never varied, the total circled and a smiling face on the back. When Ben's pockets were filled he stuffed them in the green jar he kept on his kitchen counter—a gift from a former girlfriend for some ridiculous occasion. A one month anniversary or some other trivial thing.

Ben couldn't go wrong at work, and he was happy that Anna seemed to have fallen under the same magic spell of success. One night, after they had enjoyed plates of pasta and a tasty green salad at the kitchen table of his tiny apartment, he looked at her and knew what he needed to make his life perfect.

"Anna, will you move in with me?"

She turned from the sink. The huge grin on her usually composed face answered his question. He pulled her into his arms. His chin rested on her head as he hugged her before tipping his lips down to meet hers.

Ben loved having Anna with him. Nothing in his life had ever felt better than knowing she would be there when he came home. She didn't mind cooking and he didn't mind cleaning up, although their love for each other grew to the point that doing things side-by-side was the preferred routine. Once again, Ben was amazed at how his life had come together.

"Good morning, Margaret. Please bring me the Crypto Canning file and I'll take calls until ten o'clock. Then I want some undisturbed time."

"Okay Mr. Grigg, but Mr. Meyers asked that you call him."

"I'll get to it." The old man expected Ben to report on every minute of his time. Couldn't he see from the weekly updates that Ben was spiraling this company ever upward? Someone as competent as he was—the best this company had ever hired—shouldn't have to answer to every beck and call.

At four fifty-five Margaret reminded him that he still hadn't called Mr. Meyers. He picked up the phone. Just as he thought, the old man simply wanted to know about the Basic Concepts contract. "Progressing as planned. Sir," Ben added, knowing that this little word would keep his boss happy. After the requisite bullshit exchange, he hung up and grabbed his coat. He wanted to get home to Anna.

His apartment, perfect a month ago, was proving too small. Anna occasionally worked from home and with only one table and no desk they often dined with plates balanced on their laps. The bathroom, with its single towel rack for Ben's single towel, spilled over when Anna moved in and her things—beauty equipment was what he called it—filled the cabinet and flowed into the bedroom.

"What do you think about moving to a bigger apartment?" she asked one night.

"Fantastic idea." He watched as she folded the blanket they kept on the couch. Whenever they had time they snuggled under it, watching movies, kissing, talking, or just enjoying the warm energy of each other. At times he was frustrated that his success at work kept him late so many nights. Time with Anna was better than sitting at his desk, fantastic view of the city lights or not. A larger apartment would make her happy, so why not?

But when Anna showed him the listings, miles from the office, Ben realized he didn't want to commute.

He couldn't leave Manuel's.

"Can't you find anything around here?" As soon as the words were out of his mouth Ben realized how harsh he sounded. "I mean, maybe we can find something better in this neighborhood."

Anna sniffed at the sting of his words. "Perhaps *you* can look."

Ben heard the sniff but failed to notice the slight twitch of her eyebrow.

He found two apartments. The first was two blocks north. He

would have to veer a little out of his way each morning, but Manuel's wouldn't be much of a detour. The second was his dream come true. Twenty-fifth floor of this building. A move up, just as he had planned.

That night Ben led Anna to the elevator, having convinced the manager to loan him the key to the three bedroom luxury apartment high above them.

"Eighty-two a month is crazy in this neighborhood. Maybe closer to downtown, but here?" Anna's chin jutted and her cheek twitched.

"It's more than twice as big. You can have an office and we can have a guest room."

"Can we see the other one tonight?"

"Not until tomorrow." Ben knew the other apartment wouldn't be as good. It was only $6,700 a month.

Anna loved it.

"This view, it's unobstructed. How often does that happen?" She stood at the window and pointed. "I can catch the metro right there."

"It's farther from my office."

Anna laughed. "Like what, twenty steps? Maybe it will help you burn off that extra weight you've been complaining about."

The next day Ben wrote a check to his landlord. Sixteen thousand four hundred dollars. A deposit for the place upstairs. Thank goodness for his raise.

"How could you do that? We're in this together." Spit flew from Anna's mouth and her face was red. No subtle twitch going on today, her whole face jumped and jived.

"Anna, we were going to lose our chance. Besides, it's so much better."

"But don't you see? It's not better for me." She didn't speak to him for a week, but when the end of the month arrived she called her brother to help them carry everything into the elevator and up to the twenty-fifth floor.

Ben tapped his password into the flashing box. Pleased with his ever growing bank balance, he glanced at the memo from Mr. Meyers. Another raise. Anna really shouldn't be worried about the rent.

"Hey, do you want to go shopping tonight?" he called over his shoulder. "We can look for a mixer and a new toaster." Anna loved her morning toast, and the lever on his old toaster was taped together. Leaving it on the counter felt degrading to the gorgeous granite surfaces of their new kitchen.

Anna walked over to him, her brush gliding through her golden hair. "Sure. Dinner too?"

He wished she wouldn't walk around the house while she got ready. The long hairs scattered after her like Goldilocks's bread crumbs. Or was that Hansel and Gretel? He never remembered his fairy tales.

After steak and lobster—Ben insisted they order the most expensive thing on the menu in spite of Anna's protests—the couple browsed through the kitchenware of three department stores. Anna pointed out three mixers and two toasters, but Ben wasn't happy with them.

"Let's check out Williams Sonoma. They'll have

something." He headed toward the wide entrance to the mall.

Anna shrugged and followed.

Ben saw it as soon as he entered the luxury kitchen shop. Shiny silver arm, three colors of mixing bowls; blue the largest, yellow the smallest, and a perfect red one showing off the machine. A box full of attachments. Bread dough kneaders and cream whippers and even a food grinder. The color coordinated spatulas and spoons probably didn't come with it—just some enterprising employee's idea of a good display—but he would buy those too.

The young man who approached smiled at Ben, but addressed Anna. "Can I help you?"

"We'll take this one." Ben pointed to the emperor of all mixers.

Anna walked up to the machine and flipped the cardboard tag. Ben heard her gasp, as she turned.

"Ben, this is way too much."

This whining about money was beginning to irritate him. "I'm buying, shouldn't I be the one to decide if something is too much? I want the best. Don't you think it's right to get the best?"

"It's too big. Think of the counter space." Anna didn't stop shaking her head.

"We'll buy something to put it on." Ben pointed to a rolling cart; a butcher block, stained an unusually dark color, not the standard blond wood, and just the right size. "That'll look great in our kitchen."

"Ben, it's too much, really. I just want a hand mixer. I won't use half this stuff."

The clerk pointed to the wall. "We have some other models just over here."

Ben frowned at the guy. "This one is better, right? We'll take this one. Is that a problem?"

"No sir. I'll just get one in a box." The young man scurried away.

"And all this other stuff too," Ben called after him. "These spoons and measuring cups. I want everything that goes with it."

Once again, Ben failed to notice Anna's right cheek.

He let Anna pick out the toaster, but he couldn't stop the twinge of resentment that pinched his chest when she didn't choose the top-of-the-line model. She might insist this toaster was what she wanted, but he knew the other one was better.

Ben didn't realize how quickly the year had passed until he walked into Manuel's and saw "Mexican Latte" on the whiteboard. The fifth of May had come around again.

He set his bills and quarters on the counter.

"Happy Cinco, and a better special latte for me," he grinned at the old man. Over a year as a customer. Maybe he had earned a return smile by this time.

"Last day," Manuel mumbled.

Ben smiled. "Right. I know. Mexican Latte is only for *Cinco de Mayo*."

The old man shook his head. "Last day for..." He waved a hand around the shop and thumped his dirty apron in the middle of his chest. "Me."

Ben's grin slipped a notch. "What do you mean?"

"Is no more."

A cold chill swept over Ben. Had the old man lost his lease? "What happened? Are you moving?"

"No, just no more."

To Ben's surprise, Manuel started to laugh. A growl punctuated by sputters escaped the pale lips. The man laughed and laughed, tears streaming down his cheeks and soaking his gray beard. He picked up his pencil, circled the total and flipped over Ben's receipt. His laugh faded a bit as he completed his ritual but held an edge that made Ben clench his teeth.

Ben didn't know how to react. He always thought the barista was crazy, suspecting the sparse words that passed from those lips were not the consequence of a language issue, but a way to control the tiny kingdom he occupied.

He picked up his Mexican Latte, stuffed the receipt into his coat pocket and left the shop, shaking his head at the strange encounter.

Once outside, he stopped. He gulped the latte in spite of the burn of the liquid. Heat and spice exploded down his throat, as if he had opened his mouth to a lava spill. His heart slowed and a sense of calm came over him.

What did it matter? His life was fine, he was a successful consultant with one of the best jobs in town. In fact, definitely the best job in town. Anna had been great lately, even using the mixer after several weeks of silent boycott. And he had already bought the new toaster—the more expensive one—he would give to her in June, when her birthday came around. She would see that it really was a lot better than the one she had picked out.

Manuel and his coffee meant nothing. He wouldn't be scared by an old man's stupid tricks with a simple cup of coffee. Ben turned to toss the unfinished latte into the corner trash. This fancy drink didn't matter.

He stopped. Why waste the last bit of the heavenly liquid? He had paid for it.

In the morning Ben walked down the street hoping he had misunderstood Manuel. He could see the lowered security grate from a block away and the shop was dark. When he arrived at work Margaret brought him break-room coffee, barely warm. The next day Ben decided to take a different route. There was a Starbucks over on 182nd.

A twenty-five minute wait and he was late for work. Not that anyone kept a time clock on his departures and arrivals, but Thursdays were board meeting days and he was expected to attend.

On Friday he set his alarm for seven thirty, rather than eight o'clock. He made it to the office on time, but those Starbucks drinks had less caffeine or something because the day dragged and he dragged right along with it.

At eleven o'clock Morrison and Sons called and cancelled their contract.

At noon, behind on his work because he couldn't focus, Ben asked Margaret to order him a sandwich. The mustard stain on his white shirt could not be rinsed out and he changed into the extra shirt he kept at the office. Mr. Meyers wouldn't notice a yellow stain—the man was somewhat visually impaired—but

Henry Browning would never forgive signs of an untidy attitude. Ben stared at himself in the men's room mirror, running his hand across the five o'clock shadow on his cheek. Had he forgotten to shave this morning?

"Ben, good to see you." Meyers smiled and motioned toward the couch. This must be a casual meeting if they weren't going to use the big table to spread out files and charts.

Henry entered just as Ben took the glass of whiskey Meyers offered. He glanced at Ben, but didn't sit. "I have another meeting, so I'll be brief."

Ben's stomach churned. Maybe he should have called in sick today.

"This quarter's report wasn't good. We need to cut back. Drastically." Henry looked at Meyers and Ben saw the older partner nod.

His stomach lurched and he swallowed hard and set the empty glass on the edge of the coffee table.

"It's just the way it is, Mr. Grigg. Last hired, first—" he waved his hand and snorted. "We have to let you go."

Ben jumped up, stumbled toward the old man's desk and grabbed the wastebasket. The turkey sandwich and the whiskey hit the bottom of the metal container with a ferocious splatter, but that didn't stop Henry Browning from telling Ben he would have to leave today.

He really didn't have much to carry home. Not enough to fill the file box Margaret had conveniently placed on his desk while he was cleaning up in the bathroom. Just his crumpled dirty shirt and a cobalt blue coffee cup Anna had given him on Valentine's Day—her favorite color. Everything else belonged to the company.

Anna wasn't home when he got there—why would she be? She still had a job—so he shucked off his shoes and fell back into their bed. At six o'clock he heard her come in. He listened to her movements, knowing that she didn't know he was in the apartment. She was always first home and was usually already settled in the armchair with a book when he rushed through the door each evening.

Footsteps whispered down the hall. "Oh! You're here."

Was that disappointment in her voice? Wait until she found out about his day. Then she could be really disenchanted with him.

He didn't look at her when he told her the bad news. No need to see that dreaded twitch.

In spite of his protests Anna planned an outing for Saturday. "It will be good for you to get out. How often can we see Georgia O'Keefe without a trip to Santa Fe?"

He pulled the pillow over his head and ignored her bustling until she arrived with a tray at the bedside.

"I brought you some breakfast."

Toast, from that substandard toaster and coffee brewed in the machine she had brought with her when she moved in.

He pulled himself up and bunched the pillows behind his back. "Thanks."

Instantly the smell of the coffee overwhelmed him. His

stomach heaved and saliva pooled in his mouth because he couldn't swallow. Moving the tray to one side he ran for the bathroom.

Five minutes with his head poised over the toilet and his hands trembling.

Anna knocked. "Are you okay?"

"A bug or something," he mumbled toward the door.

"What? I can't hear you." The knob turned.

Couldn't that bitch let him puke in peace?

Ben spent the weekend in bed. Anna hovered and cooked chicken soup and kept fussing over him until he yelled and sent her off to the museum to see her blessed O'Keefe. He thought she might pout and leave him alone, but Sunday night was filled with her pathetic attempts to make him feel better.

He didn't want to feel better and he told her this in not very subtle terms. It worked because he still felt like shit on Monday morning. She hadn't made a big deal about his incompetence or asked about his severance package or even mentioned their rent was due next week. He stayed in bed as Anna dressed and left for work. At noon he untangled the sweat soaked sheets and took a shower. He needed to find another job, but couldn't wrap his mind around internet searches and phones calls to old contacts. His head was so filled with clotted thoughts that he found himself walking down 181st St toward Manuel's before he remembered it wasn't there anymore.

Ben rattled the security grate and spit on the ground. "What happened to you, you old bastard?" He kicked the metal, rattling the cage that trapped his dreams. "I need you," he yelled and grasped the wire in his hands, tugging as if he could get his coffee by brute force.

The grate rolled upward, the unexpected give sending him off balance.

It wasn't latched.

Curiosity replaced rage, and Ben quickly raised the grate and then tried the doorknob.

Not locked.

"Hello?" The shop was dim, and there was already a layer of dust on the empty counter, as if Manuel had closed his doors years ago rather than three days. "Manuel? Are you here?"

Ben's voice bounced off the walls, echoing the empty silence of a defunct business. He walked to the back of the room and opened the door to what he thought was a storage closet, but it led to a narrow alley. There was no other room in this place, just the small patch of linoleum floor and the empty coffee counter. Manuel had taken his Gaggia with him.

The old brewing machine sat on its narrow shelf, deserted for all time.

Ben glanced behind him at the open door and the street, thought about calling out once more, and didn't. He strode to the shelf in two steps, wrapped the dangling cord up and over the top of the machine and hoisted it into his arms.

It was heavier than he had expected. Ben struggled to the door.

I'm not really stealing this, he thought. Manuel left it behind. Someone else will take it if I don't.

In spite of his awkward load, Ben was able to grasp the doorknob with his fingertips and pull it closed. He couldn't manage the security grate, and left it up. There wasn't anything left for anyone to take.

"What is that?" Anna slipped out of her coat and walked into the kitchen.

"Coffee maker." Ben was working on the old brewer with rags and silver polish. He had hoped to have it shined before Anna came home, but the thing was in much worse condition than he remembered.

"You...I...do..."

He looked at Anna. "What?"

She shook her head and turned away. "Nothing."

It was almost ten o'clock when the thing was as clean as it was ever going to get. Now for the test. After a frantic search he realized they didn't have any coffee in the apartment. Anna was in bed, so he grabbed his coat and went out. If he hurried he could make it to the mini-mart on 190th before they closed.

Mini-marts don't carry much in the way of coffee. One choice, the red plastic container filled with highly processed stuff which resembled coffee in that it was brown and ground. Ben knew it wouldn't be Manuel's coffee. He just wanted to see if the machine worked.

Work it did. With a puff and a grumble and a gurgle, Ben brewed his first pot. Grinning with success he poured the pale liquid into a mug.

He spit the mouthful of bitter coffee back into the mug. He

would have to work on the ratio of coffee to water. Tomorrow he would shop for beans.

A week later Ben took the subway across town to Specialty Java for the third time. Arabica from Ethiopia. Robusta beans from Peru. He'd tried nearly all of the varieties the store carried. So far the Jamaican was the closest to Manuel's wonderful brew, but not quite. He paid for the beans and hurried home.

"Any luck on the job search?"

Anna's snide tone pierced his temple like a tribal hatchet. He hadn't guessed that she would turn into an old fishwife. He cursed himself for asking her to move in.

"Lay off will you?" He carefully measured the ground Arabica into the brew basket. Seven level scoops. Maybe he needed to brew a full pot to get the same flavor Manuel had conjured up. He was home all day so it wouldn't go to waste.

Why hadn't he pushed the barista to explain what those extra quarters delivered? He thought about trying to find the old man, but he didn't even know his last name. Maybe the city had records on business permits? He searched the web to no avail.

It took Ben a month to come close to Manuel's perfect brew. A mixture of three grinds, each from a different corner of the city, left him mellow and content. He stayed in bed until Anna left, then took his time measuring, adding the filtered water and gazing out the kitchen window while the aroma of the coffee filled the air. He usually sat out on the balcony while he drank his masterpiece, but today was sunny and the blue sky urged him to get outdoors. Filling a travel mug, he pulled on his cap and set out.

A white truck stood at the curb in front of Manuel's place. Ben's chest tightened as he rushed down the empty sidewalk. If Manuel was back things would change. He would find a job, Anna would smile at him, and life would be good.

The old counter had been removed and the dirty walls glowed with fresh lemon colored paint. Two men kneeled, gluing fake hardwood boards into place directly over the old linoleum.

"What's the deal?" Ben asked. "Is Manuel back?"

The younger of the two, his red beard so full it pressed against his chest, shook his head. "No, man. Lease improvements."

"What's it gonna be?" Ben's heart settled back to its normal beat.

"Nothing yet. The owner couldn't find a tenant so he's jazzing it up a bit."

"Can it. We got work to do." The older man flipped his chin toward the door. "Sorry dude, but you really shouldn't be in here."

"Got it." Ben frowned and headed out.

The day was still fine, in spite of the fact that Manuel wasn't back. Ben finished his coffee and went to the park, the empty travel mug working as a baton as he set his pace at an easy jog. Maybe he didn't have a job, but something was just around the corner for him, he could feel it.

That night he reassured Anna that he would pay her back for his portion of the rent he had missed.

"Really Ben? And how do you plan to do that? With this mystery job that's going to fall from the sky? Jobs come to those who apply. And send out resumes. And go for interviews." She slammed her fork onto the table. "We need to figure this out. The Bank of Anna is closed, depleted, debunked, de-...de-..."

He felt her anger fizzle into something worse. Despair. Discouragement. "I know, Babe. Really, it's just around the corner. I can feel it."

"That's not good enough, Ben. You've been singing that song too long. Show me the offer, not some mystical aura that you seem to think gathers around your head."

"Tomorrow. I'll show you something tomorrow, I swear." He smiled and moved to kiss her, but she turned her face away and his lips awkwardly brushed her ear.

Ben jumped out of bed when Anna's six thirty alarm jangled its Bill Wither's melody. He beat her to the kitchen and scooped coffee into the brewer's basket. He would show her that he meant what he said.

"Here you go." He presented her favorite blue mug filled with his Jamaican/Peruvian/Hawaiian blend, a touch of half and half and a dash of cinnamon completing the offering.

"You're up early." She reached for the mug, blew on it, and took a sip. "Hey, this is really good."

"Better than that office stuff you settle for." Ben grinned. "Today, I promise. Today I find a job."

She raised her eyebrows and twisted her lips. "Good."

Just the hint of a twitch.

As soon as Anna picked up her briefcase and left, Ben jumped into the shower. Last night, as he was fighting insomnia, an idea had formed and today he would make it happen.

The two workmen were gone. The old grate had been replaced with a new one, closed and locked tight. That didn't bother Ben because he found what he needed on the green sign leaning in the window.

For lease. Followed by a phone number.

A quick call, a trip downtown, a successful conversation with his brother about a short term loan, and Ben had good news to take home to Anna. He cleaned the kitchen, vacuumed and brewed more coffee—decaf—while he waited for her to come home.

"You look happy." She draped her coat over the back of the couch. "Good news?"

"You bet. I told you today would be my lucky day. You're looking at the owner of the New Manuel's Coffee and More." He kept his next thought to himself. He'd be the proud owner once the business paperwork was completed and he found someone to loan him a bit more money.

"What?"

Ben smiled and nodded. "Yep. I'm my own boss from now on."

"But Ben..." Anna paused. "You found the old guy? You paid him for his business? A defunct business?"

"I'm starting from scratch. I don't need him. You tasted my coffee. I'm good, baby, as good as he ever was. Better."

"I...it's just...how are we going to pay the rent?

"I'm serious about this. I'm not stupid. I get it; businesses take a while to generate income." Did she really think he was that naive? "Crane is loaning me some money."

"Your brother? You convinced him to do that? Did you lie to him or what?"

Ben felt irritation brewing deep inside his gut. Did Anna really think he was dishonest? She was the one pressuring him to do something. Why didn't she see that this was it, what he had been searching for all along?

"Thanks for believing in me." She hadn't even noticed the clean carpets.

After six weeks of jumping through permit and paperwork hoops, tomorrow was opening day. Ben had spent the evening at the new shop putting in the final touches and Anna was asleep when he got home. He would draw a bigger crowd than Manuel, but the place really was too tiny for tables and chairs. A few stools at a counter he had built along the wall would have to suffice. The old brewer had been installed on a new shelf in the back corner. The Gaggia—he had found a used one on-line—filled the center of the room on a counter built to look like a tree stump. He had paid a starving artist to add birds and jungle-like trees to the yellow walls. His Mexican latte would beat Manuel's any day of the week. You wouldn't have to wait until May to feel the pull of the Mayan spirits.

Ben's pride and joy—a six foot whiteboard—was mounted on the back wall. Bigger than Manuel's propped-up sign, his menu would be visible from the street. Ben decorated the edges with blue and yellow daisies, the only flower he knew how to draw, before carefully printing out his offerings. Coffee $3, Cappuccino $5/5^{25}, Mocha $4^{75}/5, Latte $4^{50}/4^{75}, Mexican Latte $6/6^{25}.

He was on his way before Anna ever woke up, shaking off his disappointment that she didn't get up to wish him well.

"So what's with the twenty-five cents more? Extra shot?" The young man's beard was neatly trimmed into a sharp point and Ben recognized the guy's suit as a six-thousand-dollar Brioni.

"It's better."

"What the hell does that mean?"

"Try it. It really is better."

"You're crazy man. You think I'm going to fork over an extra quarter a day just because you say so? Tell you what, I'll give you fifty-cents for an extra shot and we'll call it a day."

Ben shrugged. His third day in business and he had yet to convince even one of the steady stream of customers to take his word that it could be better.

He sipped the deluxe version. Maybe he couldn't convince them because he had yet to convince himself. What had Manuel added to make him feel on top of the world every day? He pictured the pitcher of muddy brown liquid. Crack? Some secret Hispanic ingredient that imitated meth? He should be happy that this crowd seemed to like his coffee, returning every day, but until he could learn the secret his abundant daily receipts meant only that he could work toward repaying his loans.

After a week in business Ben settled into a routine. He loved walking down the dark street at five in the morning, unlocking the grate, and starting up the machines. He had a jump on the rest of the city, but not a jump toward the frantic world that woke up at seven o'clock. Ben had the pleasure of the chirping birds and still air and peace not apparent any other time of day. Evenings were different, but he enjoyed them as well. Turning around the "Come On In" sign to his cleverly worded "See You Tomorrow," cleaning the old brewer, wiping down his counters, and mopping his floor, made him smile and whistle.

His only regret was that Anna hadn't come to see the shop. Not even once. "Work is crazy" or "Errands today" were her thinly veiled excuses. Even with these warning signs Ben was shocked when he came home on Friday to see suitcases next to the door.

"Babe?" he called out and rushed to the kitchen.

His wool Burberry was draped over his chair. The luggage took on a new meaning. She wasn't leaving, she was kicking him out.

"Anna, please, you—"

The flat palm of her hand held up like a primary school crossing guard stopped him.

"I found something. I think you should take a look." She held out a small piece of paper—no, a receipt. Ben took it from her.

$6.75. His last coffee at Manuel's. Ben flashed back on crumpling the paper and stuffing it into his pocket. The pocket of his Burberry.

"What?" He squinted at Anna.

"Turn it over."

The image of the old barista's crazy laughter and the pencil in his hand came back to Ben. He turned the receipt, expecting the usual circle, eyes, and slash of a smile. There was something written on the back.

Not better. All is the same.

What did that mean? Ben pictured Manuel smiling and shaking his head, then laughing. He smelled the coffee, felt the old linoleum under his feet. He hadn't imagined things. They had been better. And when Manuel left they most certainly had been worse.

A black hole opened in Ben's chest. A hole filled with the darkest roast and the aroma of bitter beans.

THE MASK

There is no disguise so clever you can hide from yourself. I know, because I have been wearing them for the last sixty years. And I haven't celebrated Halloween since donning my mask.

The first disguise I wore was that of dedicated student. I diligently poured over my books each night: Algebra, US History, Advanced Placement English. Nothing could tear me away from my studies. But it's not like anyone invited me to leave them. In between essays and mid-terms I covered myself with the gossamer shield of vocabulary. I used words as a veil to keep everyone from seeing who I was. The other high school students—particularly those attracted to four letter words—sneered at me when I opened my mouth. My obscure literary references, my use of words better left to writers of a previous century, and the huge stack of books I carried everywhere created a disguise which completely covered my hatred and anger. There were no slumber parties, no boyfriends, no camping trips with a BFF. But I didn't need a Best Friend, and Forever was such a long time. The mask had a serious, thin-lipped smile.

Shy, like someone who didn't want to flaunt their smarts, but my new face was smug in hidden confidence. My faded blue eyes said I AM smart and I will stay that way.

"Our Peggy will go to any college she wants," my father bragged to his friends.

"Peg has her head screwed on straight, not like me," my older brother told his new wife.

"Margaret Black, you have been picked as valedictorian," the school counselor announced.

Once on stage for that terrible ceremony, delivering a speech I had copied from an online site—my own words hadn't felt good enough—I realized that the exposure picked away at my disguise. Standing in front of others pulled at the tiny threads that held everything together. So when I moved on to college I changed my costume.

Wallflower. Shy and maybe a little wanting in the brains department, but she does well when she studies. That is how my professors saw me. There were a few problems: my roommate wouldn't give up on my love life and my English professor wanted to be a mentor to me. So I adjusted the cloak I wore.

"I'm not interested in men," I told Sandy.

"I can fix you up with a woman," she jumped off her bed and grabbed her phone. "In fact, I know the perfect girl for you."

"Stop. I'm not interested in women either."

"Come on, Peggy Sue. You can't think that a tiny bit of fun would keep you from your perfect grades."

I shuddered. Sandy used every variation of Margaret. She seemed to think changing my name daily was cute. Peggy Sue had to be the worst.

She moved close to me, too close, and spoke in a whining voice. "Just one night. That's all I'm asking."

I was tempted. I felt the mask slip, my real eyes uncovered for a moment. It might be fun to go out with Sandy and her friends.

"We're going to move Karla's car. It takes a crowd to lift it, but it will serve her right when she can't find it. She's such a bitch."

A memory sprang forth from the depths of my mind and slammed into me. The image of six girls, circled around me, faces distorted into huge red mouths, swam before my eyes. I pushed the mask back into place. "No, I can't. I have a paper due tomorrow."

After four years, my disguise was stripped from me by nothing more than an endless ceremony with long-winded speakers, a walk down an aisle in a heavy robe, and a luncheon with a few interested relatives who handed me sealed envelopes along with their mumbled congratulations.

For two weeks I ran naked. I moved my sparse belongings back to the pink bedroom, which although still pink now served as my parent's guest room as well as my mother's sewing room. I ventured out only far enough to eat and fill out job applications.

Then I got the phone call. I was top candidate. I could hide as a journalist intern with The Mercury. I packed my bags and moved into a small apartment.

This job called for a new disguise. I found that my written

words could not only shield me, they could distract the enemy. Meg Grayson, my byline read. A made-up name to go with my disguise.

I didn't have to deny myself. *I* didn't have to date, but Meg Grayson could date. *I* could be depressed but Meg could laugh and flirt and be happy.

Margaret Black could stay at home and hide.

The mask almost slipped again when Meg fell in love. She was close to saying yes when George Price asked for her hand.

Two weeks of nightmares stopped her. Two weeks of the six faces, the taunts, the spitting, and the sneers. Two weeks of painful memories rising to the surface once more.

Margaret pulled the mask back into place. In a timely way, an offer for a syndicated column at a New York paper forced Meg to move far away from George Price and his offer of love.

Margaret Black nearly disappeared. I had become Meg. The disguise was now tattooed on my skin, no cloak needed. Meg won awards, traveled, and wrote more columns. She wasn't afraid of standing in front of the crowd, the mask so firmly adhered to her face there was no chance of it slipping. She worked in museums and helped foster children. She planted a rooftop garden and ate fresh vegetables. She rarely stayed home. And she didn't retire. Writing a gossip column was something even an old lady could manage.

When I was seventy-three years old I had a stroke. My right hand, the hand that had written years of words that have protected me, failed. The mask slipped and Meg faded.

My parents and my brother were long dead. There was no one to call. The doctor arranged for me to move to Sunset Heights.

Really? Sunset Heights? I would rather jump from a cliff and end my suffering.

I didn't recover from the damage. My arm withered and my disguise grew thin. The legs that had worked so hard to support me in spite of the shrunken left limb I had been born with gave up altogether. For months I lay in the lumpy bed day and night, immune to the wonderful things Sunset Heights had to offer: bingo and country western music and stringing beads.

Although I kept my eyes closed and tried to pull the mask on tight, I couldn't keep out the visions. I couldn't hide from the memories and they seemed as real as if the whole thing hadn't happened a life time ago.

The six girls. Danielle, Barbara, Carol, Karen, Debbie and Laura. They had surrounded me. Their fourteen-year-old tongues were as sharp as Japanese Samurai swords.

"Hey Peg Leg. We got a costume for you so you can come to the Halloween party tonight. We need a lame donkey."

"Don't ask John to carry your stuff anymore. He's my brother and I don't want to live with a contaminated person."

"Do you ever wish you had died at birth? Probably would have been better then limping around all your life."

Their hissing voices surrounded me and although I knew I should stand up to them, I was tired and my leg didn't work at all when I was stressed. I tried to limp off, away from their torment, but they circled.

Wolves.

I slumped to the ground with my arms over my head.

Danielle didn't like that. She kicked me and laughed.

"Stop", I yelled, but only in my head. The words never reached my lips.

Laura spat on me.

I sobbed, maybe for hours. I don't know how long they kept up their hissing and spitting and kicking, but I came home bruised and dirty. I slipped quietly into the bathroom and washed away the rage that wanted to take over. A furious volcano burned inside my crippled body. As I dried off with one of the soft towels my mother was so proud of, I looked away from the mirror. I sat on the toilet and tried to think, tried to plan, tried to see a way out of this life.

The next day I put on the disguise.

Suddenly now, nearly sixty years later, I could see the price I had paid for wearing the cloak of denial. The rage I had pushed down bubbled up, the volcano only dormant for all this time, never extinguished. My mask hadn't been that of a smart girl. Only someone in hiding. Someone who hadn't ever lived.

Meg, that bitch. She had taken away everything. It wasn't Danielle or Laura or any of the others. It was Meg. Moving, changing jobs, saying no to offers of vacations or concerts or marriage.

Or love.

I reached up and pulled the tubes out of my nose.

Pulling out the tubes hadn't worked because they simply

switched to this mask which bunched up on my chin and pinched.

"Maggie May, my love. Don't you know if you keep pulling off the mask we'll have to tie your hands?" The nurse, the sweet one, placed the rubber jelly fish back over my mouth and nose. My skin was thin and everything hurt.

She smiled and patted my arm. "Much better now, right my pretty Maggie?" She didn't wait for a reply, but turned and left, her sensible shoes squeaking across the vinyl floor.

As soon as I saw the last of her, I pulled the mask from my face. I took a deep breath of the stale air, my nose still working enough to take in the odor of urine and old age. Soon, I told myself, soon you will smell nothing but fresh baked bread and honeysuckle. I turned my head to the door, to the ghost of the hurried nurse.

"My name is Margaret."

Management

Kimberly Martin couldn't believe the blue coat was gone. She never lost things—her careful method of alphabetization and color coding helped her to track her precious belongings. The blue coat always hung just between the black sweater and the burgundy velveteen dress she wore to church each Sunday.

She had worn the coat to work, where all employees were required to hang anything larger than a sweater on wall hooks in the break room.

"Stupid rule," she mumbled as she looked around the cubicles. Management had decided that coats draped over chairs or the five foot walls wasn't professional.

A thief was among the ten typists, seven transcribers and fourteen data entry technicians who shared the office space.

Kimberly cruised around the room like the coast guard on patrol, looking into the islands of workers formed by the placement of the moveable walls. Management was constantly reorganizing the work space. More efficient in clusters one year and less chat in rows the next. This was completed without the input of the humans who actually worked in these pods, as if managing the employees was some sort of global regulatory task. She peered into each doorway and stood on tiptoe while glancing over the tops of the walls.

No flash of cerulean blue polyester—it could have been silk, but who can afford that—a fabric so shiny it gleamed like a jewel. Not an easy coat to steal. Whoever had it must have stuffed it in a file drawer or taken it to their car. It wasn't meant to be crumpled. The silky fabric would crease and a trip to the dry cleaner was the only thing that could bring it back to its flawless state.

Kimberly stood in front of Mr. Grant's office. A real room with a door, although the front wall was glass and if he wanted privacy he had to draw his blinds. Even the top dog at Efficiency Incorporated didn't have a window to the outside world, so drawing his blinds enclosed him in a ten by ten cell. Not that Mr. Grant was top dog. They resided somewhere else.

The blinds were open and he plastered a smile on his face and waved her in.

"Kim, what can I do for you?"

"Someone stole my new coat."

The artificial upturn on his lips flipped into a frown. His brow crunched into an "oh no not again" wrinkle.

He considered her a difficult employee, she knew that. But her complaints were valid. The heater vent did blow directly on her chair. Marsha Peters didn't clean up after she cooked lasagne that exploded and left the bloody splatter of a tomato sauce murder all over the inside of the microwave. The laminating machine was outdated and left air bubbles in documents that deserved to be covered in a wrinkle-free coating.

And Greg Bloom had touched her inappropriately, no matter how much he denied it. While she might not have been able to prove his hand had rubbed her backside in the copy room, others had stepped forward to corroborate his sexist comments.

Well…anyway…Patsy Banks had agreed that Greg once told an off color joke, but wasn't that sexist? It had been a joke about men in a bar.

Mr. Grant tapped his pen against a stack of manilla folders. *Tap, tap, tap.* Kimberly waited. Wasn't he going to do anything? *Tap, tap, tap.*

"My mother gave me the coat for Christmas." She choked out the words.

"So it's not a new coat?" *Tap, tap.*

Oh no. She forgot that Mr. Grant knew Mother had died last year. How did she explain to her boss that she had bought the coat for herself, wrapped it in candy cane paper, topped with a gift card inscribed *With love from Mother* and placed it under her own tree? That she couldn't bear the thought of a Christmas all by herself and no one had thought to invite her over for the day?

"She bought it for me before she died. It was wrapped so I waited until Christmas to open it. A new coat. That someone has taken from those very un-secure hooks where you insist we leave our valuable possessions."

"I'm sure it will turn up." He opened the file he had tapped to death.

"That's all you have to say?"

The sound of the air which puffed from his nose was like a

slap in the face. He turned to look at the painting of a meadow on his wall. "I'll see what I can do, Miss Martin."

Kimberly sputtered, then sighed. It was just like everything else in this office. She was brushed aside like unwanted cat fur. At least he hadn't called her Kim again.

The next day she sat in her car, watching the back door of Efficiency Incorporated through which all employees must enter. Another one of Management's rules. This wasn't Victorian England, a servant's entrance separate from the noble front door. Efficiency Incorporated wasn't a drop-in business, with clients walking in to hire them. As far as she could tell no one used the front door except the Fed Ex man. All clients were contract work found over the internet, or signed during business lunches at swanky restaurants with breathtaking views. She knew this because her old boss, Franklin Green, once took her along. Of course, that was fifteen years ago when she was first hired.

She never did figure out why she had been invited. Not to take notes, as she had assumed. He never asked her to do anything more than sit and listen, enjoying the scampi and glass of white wine he ordered for her. It had been a test for a promotion.

A test which she had failed.

But now, here, with all the new rules, she knew that the thief would have to enter through the back door.

"You're late." Roberta Fasma, her supervisor, held a stack of files.

"Sorry, just…overslept." Kimberly slipped her purse into the locking file drawer under the counter that served as a desk in these cubicles. She wasn't wearing a coat today, although it was forty-seven degrees out this morning.

"Mr. Grant would like these typed by nine forty-five."

Kimberly powered up her computer and glanced through the files. Of course whoever stole the coat wouldn't have worn it. Waiting by the back door had been a stupid plan.

Backspace, highlight, insert symbol. Kimberly could type and plot with ease.

What if she set a trap? She could bring something valuable, but not too valuable, and leave it on her desk. Hidden camera to catch the thief in the act.

Her fingers stopped, poised mid-strike above the keyboard. She had forgotten all about those security cameras up in the rafters of the open ceiling.

This building had been a roller skating rink before children took to riding those skateboards on the streets and it went out of business. When converted to offices, the high ceiling space was left open. Maybe to keep the busy worker bees in their cubicles from feeling claustrophobic. More likely because it saved money.

There were small boxes up there, painted dark green to match the air ducts that clung to the beams—also green—as if to pretend they worked in a forest instead of a building. Those boxes were cameras.

Kimberly jumped from her chair and ran to Mr. Grant's office.

"They might show who stole my coat," Kimberly gasped as

she flung open her boss's door.

"Kimberly." Mr. Grant's voice was stern. "I'm in the middle of a meeting."

He was. With Bonnie Fuller, who sat in a chair pulled close to his. The woman's cheeks flushed a mottled pink and her tongue darted out like a reptile, smoothing over her red lips.

Kimberly had failed to notice Mr. Grant's blinds were closed.

"It's just...the security cameras. They'll show who stole my coat." Kimberly backed toward the door. Bonnie was staring down at her fingernails, as if they were the most important thing in the world.

"We can talk about this later."

Kimberly walked back to her desk, mulling over the strange feeling drifting around in the back of her throat, her breath in short puffs, maybe of anger, maybe because she wasn't in the habit of running anywhere these days.

The following morning Kimberly went straight to Mr. Grant's office. His blinds were closed so she knocked.

"What is it?" He didn't sound all that busy.

"Mr. Grant. It's me. Kimberly Martin." She put her hand on the doorknob only to have her arm nearly pulled from its socket as the door swung inward.

Her boss stood in the doorway and frowned. "I'm busy, Miss Martin. I thought you understood a closed door means do not disturb."

"I'm sorry Mr. Grant. It's just...I didn't sleep all night

thinking about my coat. Did you review the security tapes?"

"Enough about the coat. If it was so valuable, why did you wear it to work? You knew it would hang in the break room. No more of this, Miss Martin. The subject is closed."

Kimberly gasped as he slammed the door. Not because he had been so terribly rude—although he had been terribly rude—but because she caught a glimpse of Bonnie Fuller's back and she could swear the woman was buttoning up her blouse.

"I must speak to Management." Kimberly stood before Roberta's desk and twisted a small lace hankie. She dabbed her eyes for good measure.

"Who?" Roberta glanced up from the yellow notepad on which she vigorously scribbled tight, quick notes.

"Management."

"I heard you. But who in management?"

"Why..." Kimberly paused. She didn't know who was responsible for what. All those offices—with doors and walls—scattered around the edge of the building, as well as some distant office, probably in a different city, which held the people really in control. "The member of Management who is in charge of the coat hooks."

Roberta sighed and set her pen on top of the notepad. "Why don't you tell me what you really need."

"I need to watch the security footage."

"And you need to do this because?" Roberta raised her eyebrows.

"Because Mr. Grant refused to take the theft of my blue coat seriously. He was very rude to me as well. That's against the rules, isn't it? To treat an employee that way?" Kimberly sniffed and let her lower lip quiver just a bit. "On second thought maybe I need to talk to the part of Management who deals with how I'm treated around here."

"Kimberly, you really need to come to me first. I'm your supervisor, remember? Mr. Grant...isn't...it's not his job..." Roberta paused. "Just come to me. We've been over this before."

"You weren't here."

"When?"

"When my coat was stolen. It was Monday. You were out. Sick, I suppose."

Roberta sighed. "I'm very sorry you lost—"

"Not lost. Stolen."

"I'm sorry your coat is missing. I'll see what I can do."

Kimberly fretted all weekend. She had a ticket to *My Fair Lady* at The Old Playhouse. The elegant cerulean coat was just the thing for a night out. She could barely focus on singing along with the songs, her mind filled with wondering what the security tapes would show.

But on Monday when she made her way straight to Roberta's desk, nothing had been done.

"This isn't acceptable. What do I have to do? Call the police? File an official report to start the investigation?" She didn't wait for Roberta—who obviously did not take her job or her promises seriously—to answer.

No, Kimberly marched to Mr. Grant's office, where the

blinds and the door were both open, although nothing would have stopped her at this point.

She stepped inside and closed the door.

"Mr. Grant. I know what you're doing and I'm going straight to Management and telling them, unless you give me access to those security tapes by...three o'clock today." She was being generous because for all she knew it would only take him two minutes and three clicks on his computer to access the footage. "Miss Bonnie Fuller is probably up for promotion soon if I'm not mistaken."

Mr. Grant's face turned that purplish shade of red that Kimberly thought was a sign of impending heart attack. What was it old fashion novels called it? Apocalyptic fit? Or maybe it was apoplectic? Anyway, she had definitely gotten through to him.

"Come with me. Now." Mr. Grant sputtered as he made his way through the maze of cubicles to her desk. He leaned over her keyboard, typed and clicked and then walked away without another word.

It had taken him less than two minutes to access the files.

At five thirty Kimberly slammed her laptop closed. It hadn't taken her long to figure out how to scan through the security tapes. The problem was that the cameras were on a cycle. Sixty seconds in ten areas. No continuous footage in the break room. So one minute her coat was there, the shiny blue visible even on the black and white video, and then the camera switched to shots of the hallway, the back door, the front entrance, and six other random areas. Then back to the break room and no coat. It could only mean that the thief had knowledge of the cycling cameras.

The next day she had a new plan. She would insist that Mr. Grant open an official investigation. One with police involvement. They would figure out who knew about the cameras and they would search the suspect's house. They could even test the hook for fingerprints. Anyone other than her would be the thief, since she always hung her wraps on the third hook.

But when she got inside the building and walked to her desk, Roberta was standing there, arms folded across her chest.

"Miss Martin, I'm sorry to inform you that your services are no longer needed at Efficiency Incorporated."

Kimberly squinted and shook her head. "What are you talking about?"

"You are relieved of your position due to unacceptable behaviors. Effective immediately."

Fired? They couldn't do that, she knew her rights. "You're kidding, right? What about my notice, my seniority, my....my warning meetings?"

Roberta picked up a folder which Kimberly hadn't noticed. "It's all in here. Documented meetings. Multiple attempts to communicate to you the expected protocols, procedures, the way things are required."

Kimberly stared at the folder.

Roberta pointed to a cardboard file box next to her chair. "Please take your personal belongings and I will escort you from the building."

It was a numb drive home, the box tipping off the seat when she turned left on Madison and spilling the four things which constituted her personal belongings—a pencil holder, a staple remover shaped like an iris and a cloth placemat useful for eating lunch at her desk, and a blue mug—on to the floor. As soon as she was home Kimberly made three phone calls. One to her friend Marsha who had lost her job ten years ago, one to the worker's comp office and one to an employment call center. Marsha wasn't home, so she left a message. The man at the worker's comp office told her she really didn't have a case and suggested she file for unemployment. Although, he added, if she had been fired it wasn't likely she qualified. The employment call center directed her to their website, where she found three jobs for which she considered turning in an application.

It was Mr. Grant, of course. She had been blind to think he would cave so easily. There had to be recourse—a lawsuit, a wrongful termination charge—something she could do.

When she hired an attorney things got ugly. Mr. Grant denied any relationship with Bonnie Fuller and of course Bonnie Fuller backed him up. It was brought to light that Kimberly had falsely accused other men of sexual harassment during her time at Efficiency Incorporated. The long lists of her complaints—at least one a week for seven years—was faxed to her lawyer. He shook his head and suggested she quit wasting her money and his time and move on with her life.

She took his advice, although only to work on another plan.

Mr. Grant would not get away with this. She would think of something.

It is a good thing that time tends to dull anger. The year passed and Kimberly was busy at her new job with the Markell Inspection Agency. She enjoyed the work, checking over protocol for compliance with Federal Regulations, and the thoughts of Mr. Grant faded.

It was Thanksgiving when the blue coat entered her mind. She had been invited to Cara Scantly's house for dinner. She dressed with care—it wasn't every day someone invited her anywhere—and as she put on her new black coat she felt a tiny pang of sadness at the absence of the blue coat.

"Wine. I need to stop for wine. And flowers." She had to go a bit out of her way, but she hadn't thought about bringing anything until now.

As Kimberly pulled into the driveway of the strip mall on the corner of 10th and Madison she caught a flash of blue from the corner of her eye. She slammed on the brakes and was rewarded with the blast of several horns.

"Okay, okay. I'm going." She pulled forward, feeling silly for imagining she had seen her coat. But not so silly that she didn't pull her car into the parking slot beside *The Lounge*, an upscale restaurant known for its specialty Thanksgiving meals. She had actually considered coming here herself. Although she was used to doing things alone now—over two years since Mother had passed—she didn't like the idea of a holiday dinner alone. She had been saved from that decision by Cara's invitation.

There *was* someone in a blue coat. It hadn't been her imagination at all. The same cerulean she had fallen in love with before.

Kimberly's heart raced and she held her breath as she watched the woman turn. But it wasn't the woman she recognized first. No, her mind didn't process who this was until after she identified Mr. Grant as the man holding open the door for the lady.

Bonnie Fuller was wearing Kimberly's coat.

MADAM S

The woman was stunning. Mark couldn't believe he was attracted to her, because she wasn't young. He found it difficult to tell how old she might be, but well past his thirty-two years.

Generally he was attracted to very young women, but she had to be what people meant when they said "a timeless beauty."

"Hello." A smooth whisper slipped off her lips and floated through a thick sea of thoughts as it found its way to his ear.

"I haven't seen you here before," he said, immediately regretting how trivial the line sounded. He came to the bar every night after work and stayed for hours. The amber liquids he downed well into the evening where the only thing that kept him sane.

He let her think it was her idea she come home with him.

He slept with her. In the cliché sense.

And this thing—this relationship—which would have made him gag with disgust only six days earlier, blossomed.

He tried to tell his friends about her.

"Mark, this has to be some kind of mother complex." James

rolled his eyes.

"Nope," Steven added, "from what I've seen of her, it's a grandmother complex."

"Wait." James held up a hand like a cop stopping traffic. "What is it she calls herself? Madam S? Check out his feet, guys. Cowboy boots. It's a bordello fantasy."

Snarky laughter from his buddies didn't impact him in the least.

They didn't know her soft touch as she ran her fingers down his spine. They couldn't begin to imagine her warm breath when she whispered in his ear. They were young men, used to wild sex, yelling, pumping, with blinding sweat dripping into their eyes. All they had ever known was the rampage of a SWAT team. They had never been brought to ecstasy with the subtle movements of a bomb squad technician.

He looked into her eyes. They sparkled at the edges, but melted into deep pools in the center. He felt himself fall into those pools, moving out of this world and into the next, a cool fog caressing his skin and soothing the heat that usually tormented him.

"You look so sad," she said, placing her hands on his cheeks.

"I am sad," he told her. He had always been sad, something he never understood, something his mother said was hereditary, his genes carrying the pull of despair down from great-grandfather, to son, to son, to son until they stopped here in his heart. Hungry DNA, feeding off any potential laughter and happiness whenever it could, devouring pleasure as its sustenance before he had a chance to experience the feelings.

The alcohol helped. Pumped him full of a numbing agent, made him the life of the crowd, injected his brain with quick wit and dry humor. He should have been able to push the drinking aside now that he had her to quench his thirst. But he loved the two together and didn't want to give up either one.

* * *

Jasmine sat on the bench and closed her eyes, letting the sun warm her face. She never heard the woman until she spoke, mere inches from her ear.

"It's a shame to be alone on such a beautiful day."

Jasmine choked and jumped up, adrenaline blasting her heart into Olympic-strength pounding.

"Excuse me. I didn't mean to scare you. You just looked so lonely, sitting here without your friend."

Jasmine supposed the woman was in her late fifties, based on the streaks of gray in her forelock and the wrinkles around her eyes. She wore an old-fashioned cashmere sweater with pearl buttons and a gray wool skirt. Like someone from a different century.

"You watch us? That's creepy."

The stalker threw back her head and laughed, a hollow guffaw much too loud for a park bench encounter. "I knew Mitcha. She was my friend too."

It had to be true because this strange woman pronounced Jasmine's best friend's name with the correct Meesha rather than the hard Mitch-a.

"How do you know Meesh?"

"You two always looked so stunning, sitting here. That bliss —so pure no one else in the park could ever match it. Mitcha sat here with me too." The woman patted the bench. "There should be a little bronze plaque. Dedicated to Mitcha Perez and her support of Ashford Park."

Jasmine looked away. Damn this woman for encroaching on her peace and quiet. Maybe Mitcha wasn't here today but that didn't mean she couldn't have a refreshing, peaceful lunch break. She didn't want to encourage conversation, but she couldn't hold her tongue. "I don't think she ever actually gave any money to the park."

The woman leaned forward, as if determined that Jasmine look at her. "No, you're spot on about that. She is saving every dime for herself. Don't you think that's part of why she took that new job? She chose the cash over her time with you."

Jasmine was silent.

"Anyway, I'm here now. I'll keep you company so you don't have to sit alone. Everything is so much better when shared, don't you think? And you don't really have anyone else."

Jasmine snorted and half turned. "You don't even know me. Why are you saying these things?"

"I do know you. I know that your mother hasn't called in weeks and has never even bothered to come see you. Ten years living in L.A., it's not like she can't afford it. Retired and all that life insurance money? Only a short plane trip? No, it's clear she has no interest in visiting."

Jasmine glanced at her watch. "Sorry, my lunch break is

over. It's been—"

"And we both know you'll never be sitting here with a nice young man, don't we? Of course that's why she won't come visit." The terrible woman laughed again.

The sound hurt Jasmine's teeth with its grating bellow. She stood to leave. She hadn't planned on giving the crazy lady a second glance but she turned and faced her. "I can't believe you are any friend of Mitcha. You are rude and...invasive...and..."

A gray wave flowed over the woman's face and her colorless eyes glowed. Jasmine took a step back. Should she pinch herself? See if this was a dream? A dream in which a zombie came to the park to creep her out?

"I used to be her friend. You'll see, my dear. Mitcha is as fickle as they come. You're alone now and you might as well accept it."

* * *

Jack wiped the sweat off his forehead with the red hand towel he had tied to his golf bag. "How about another nine?" he asked Peter.

"No way. I can't keep up this pace. Not in ninety degree heat." Peter looked toward the clubhouse. "A crisp G and T for me. Have you tried the new tonic yet? Marcos orders it special. Something different about it, a zing to it."

Jack smiled and shook his head. "I'm not ready to go in. I'll hit a few more and catch up with you later." Jack was a recovering—make that recovered—alcoholic. It was one of the hardest things about being a member of the Crystal Lake Golf and Racquet Club. Lots of people to play tennis with or hit a round, but they always wanted cocktails afterwards.

At seventy-three, Jack was fit. He worked hard to keep his weight in line and his joints limber. Ten years ago things hadn't been so easy for him. A workaholic, his blood pressure was elevated and his body flabby. Work wasn't the only thing he had been addicted to—booze had been his best friend. Well, at the time he believed that was true. It was only after Karen died and he retired that he realized he was drowning in drink.

He put an end to that after a four day blackout. It was one thing to live in an alcohol haze when you had a wife. Quite another to lose ninety-six hours of time when you were alone. The cigarette burns on his sofa had attested to how close he came to eliminating himself along with everything he owned.

After Jack hit the requisite two buckets of balls, he headed into the clubhouse. He could get a sandwich and sit with the others. The food would distract him from the fact that there would be no drink in front of him.

Peter and Gloria were sitting with a group and he joined them.

"Hey, here's the man!" Peter had obviously made good his promise of that gin and tonic. More than one if the volume of his voice was any measure.

"Jack," Peter's trophy wife Gloria smiled. "Good to see you. You know everyone, right?" She waved at the others gathered around the low glass table. The club favored oversized leather couches and chairs.

Jack looked around at the group as he found a seat with a clear shot at the table. He set his plate down and nodded. "Think so. Parker, Smith." He dipped his chin to greet the others.

"I don't think we've had the pleasure." A salt-and-pepper haired woman with clear blue eyes reached across the table. "Jack, is it?"

"Yes. Hello." He leaned forward and returned her handshake, waiting for her to offer her vital statistics.

Marcos interrupted. "Can I get anyone another round?" Jack realized that he was blocking the waiter's access to the table.

The blue-eyed woman didn't let go of his hand. Awkwardly, he pulled away and sat as the group called out their orders. His hand felt hot, as if her grip had seared his palm. Picking up his sandwich he took a bite. Her unrelenting gaze left him feeling awkward. As if mustard were smearing his chin or he was chomping away with his mouth opened.

* * *

On Thursday Jasmine sat at her desk and stared out the window. She could see the bench from here. It was one of the reasons she and Mitcha met there every day for two years. So close to both their offices. She picked up her phone.

"You have reached Mitcha Perez. I'm sorry to miss your call. Please leave—" Meesh had gone pro. No more cute messages or funny instructions.

"Hey. It's me. A weird thing happened yesterday and I wanted to talk to you. This lady came to the park, to our bench ,and she said she was your friend—" Jasmine paused. The woman had never mentioned her name. "Anyway, can we have dinner this weekend? Or maybe spend the day on Saturday? Spring is here, we could go out to the beach. Give me a call."

On impulse Jasmine punched in another number.

"Hi Mom. It's me."

"Oh, Honey. Hi. I'm in the middle of something right now."

Her mother was always in the middle of something when she called her.

"I just—" the dead sound of the disconnect stopped her. Leave it to Mom. No *"I'll call you back"* or indication of when she might actually be available to talk to her daughter. Just cold, dark silence.

As Jasmine turned to put her phone away she glanced out the window. That woman was sitting on her bench. Before she could turn away and pretend she hadn't been looking, the old crone waved a hand. "Come on down," the gesture said. With a half smile Jasmine shook her head. The wave grew stronger and the woman smiled and patted the bench, pointing to a brown lunch bag.

Why not? Jasmine pulled her insulated lunch pouch out of her drawer. No other invitations had come her way.

* * *

Mark ordered another beer. His sixth, but who was counting? He checked the door once more. She was meeting him here after work, although the neon clock over the bar read seven-thirty and still no Madam S.

It was a strange name, like that of a woman in charge of a western hotel that housed ladies for hire.

"Come on. What does the "S" stand for? Susan? Sarah? Samantha?" he had cajoled last night, licking her salty neck. She remained smug.

It might not even be her first name. Madam Smith. Mark shook his head and sipped his beer. His concern shifted from worrying that something had happened to her—the proverbial car crash theory—to facing the fact that he had been stood up.

* * *

Jack was surprised when his phone buzzed with an unknown number. He had switched carriers last week and no one had his new information. He had disconnected his land line as well. He had grown frustrated by the number of calls for Karen. His wife had been gone for three years, for Christ's sake. She shouldn't be on anyone's call list.

"What?"

"Jack. Hello."

He didn't recognize the voice. "Who is this?"

"We never were formally introduced, were we? I was interrupted by all those golfers clamoring for more drinks."

The woman with the blue eyes. Jack smiled. Then he frowned. How did she get his number?

"I was hoping I could convince you to buy me a drink. Peter told you I'm new in town, right? I'm a social butterfly with no invitations."

This woman was certainly forward. Jack turned his hand over and looked at his palm. He could still feel the strange heat of her handshake.

"I don't...that is...how about dinner?" He didn't want to go into details about his post alcoholic state. "We can even do it tonight, if you like. But there's one thing."

"One thing?"

"How about you tell me your name so I can do this the right way?"

Her laughter bubbled through the phone line like the fizz of champagne.

"Just call me Essie."

* * *

At eleven fifty-five Jasmine glanced out the window to see if Mrs. S was out there yet. Sure enough, there she was, early as always. Her friend waved and smiled, then held up a big straw basket.

"I'll bring lunch tomorrow," she had told Jasmine yesterday. "I love to cook and now that I'm alone I never get the chance." Mrs. S didn't talk about her husband much. Jasmine didn't even know if he was dead or had simply left. Other than telling Jasmine to call her Mrs. S and a few when-I-was-young stories, the old woman didn't share much personal information.

The basket held fried chicken, potato salad, and two slices of chocolate cake. A thermos filled with hot mocha was tucked in

106

there as well.

"I know how you like your afternoon pick-me-up. Now you won't have to go out again because it's right here. Don't you think my mocha is better than theirs? It's all in the chocolate, you know. Those chain places use the cheap stuff."

"You didn't have to," Jasmine murmured as she sipped the hot drink. It was delicious but she liked the fact that Kelly and Nikki had been including her in the afternoon coffee run. She was working up the courage to invite them to have lunch with her, but Mrs. S had taken over the bench.

"I'm probably not going to be here everyday. My friends, they—" Jasmine stopped.

The expression on Mrs. S's face went from rosy pink to ashen gray. Her eyes grew moist and her chin dropped. She twisted a paper napkin until it was a tight snake.

If Jasmine could have snatched her words out of the air and stuffed them back in her mouth she would have. "But not right away. Not now anyway."

She was rewarded with Mrs. S's bright smile and a bowl of strawberries.

* * *

Mark was losing weight. His calories came only from the endless beers he downed each night, waiting to see if Madam S —The Madam, his friends had dubbed her—would actually show up. The stress of waiting burned whatever nutrition came from the grains and hops. He seldom ate any real food.

And now this. Mark was at home tonight, staring at the screen version of his credit card bill. It couldn't be right. Sure, he had started taking The Madam out to nice places for dinner. And nice places meant nice clothes, but eight thousand dollars? He scrolled through the entries. Six or more beers a night, dinner out five nights a week, and all those cover charges really added up, but the real culprit was the cash advance he had taken this month.

There was a knock on the door—her soft knock which always preceded her entry—and he shut down the computer.

"How about we stay in tonight?" He kissed her cheek and smiled.

"Whew. Your breath." She pulled away and waved her slender hand in front of her nose. Orange nails and lipstick to match.

"Sorry," he mumbled and hung his head. "It's just I'm a little short on cash right now."

The Madam smiled and pushed his shoulder. "That's what credit cards are for."

"Yeah. Right." Mark hesitated.

"Grab me a beer, will you? I'll think about what I want to do tonight while you freshen up. Mouth wash, I think. And a clean shirt."

He shrugged. "No more beers. Sorry."

She tipped her head toward the trash can next to the counter. Brown and green bottles filled it to the brim and more empties were lined up along the wall.

"Had the last one for breakfast, did you? Oh, never mind. I

have something better."

She opened her purse and pulled out a small tin. His breath must be really bad if she was going to give him a mint before he even had a chance to gargle.

It wasn't a lozenge she pulled from the container. It was a blue capsule.

"How about some water? A clean glass preferred."

He shuffled to the sink and pulled a glass from the dishes, piled high, and rinsed and filled it. When he handed it to her she shook her head and handed him the pill.

"It's not for me. It's for you."

* * *

Jack pushed the snifter aside. "Now Essie, you know I don't drink."

"Come on. Celebrate with me. I had a wonderful day in the stock market."

How did Essie have a windfall when everyone else had suffered in yesterday's crash? Jack had an appointment with his accountant tomorrow to discuss moving his IRA to cover his losses. He would be okay—his eggs weren't all in that particular basket—but thank goodness Karen wasn't around to see what a mess he had made of their finances. His kids never spoke to him, but he was pretty sure they counted on an inheritance. Both had bought big houses and new cars and went on European vacations like there was no tomorrow.

Essie picked up the brandy and dipped the tip of her finger

into the pale amber. She reached over and rubbed it on his upper lip.

Memories flooded his mind. The laughter, the weight of his troubles slipping off his shoulders, the energy, the sense he could conquer the world. He grabbed her hand and licked the rest of the liquid from her fingers, then picked up the glass.

For just a moment other memories tried to be heard. The terrible fights, the loss of his driver's license, Dr. Casco discussing the state of his liver. But the smooth liquor slipping down his throat pushed those thoughts to a place he never visited anymore, deep at the bottom of his mind.

* * *

"Jasmine, dear." Mrs. S spread a thick layer of mayonnaise on the slice of sourdough bread. "I haven't heard anything about Mitcha lately."

"Not so much mayo, please." The waistband of her favorite jeans cut into her belly. Jasmine had gained fifteen pounds in three months. None of her clothes fit anymore.

Mrs. S obligingly scraped off the mayo, leaving the bread with a very thin layer.

"Maybe a tad more than that." Jasmine didn't want her sandwich to be completely dry.

Mrs. S dipped the knife back into the jar. "Have you seen Mitcha at all?"

"No. She's probably busy with her new job."

"Not so new, dear. It's been months since she bailed on you.

Say, have you ever thought about changing jobs?"

Change jobs? Why would she want to do that? Jasmine loved her job—close to home, great benefits, good pay, and a promotion coming up soon.

Sometimes Mrs. S was just so weird.

* * *

"Waiting for The Madam again?" Steve slid onto the stool next to Mark. "Listen, man. You need to let her go."

Mark shook his head and cupped both hands around the bottle.

"No joke. You look terrible."

Steve put a hand on his shoulder and for a minute Mark remembered what it felt like to be one of the guys. Steve had been his friend for a long time.

"You're killing yourself, dude. Over an old woman."

Maybe he should kill himself. He was no longer capable of making good choices. Four warnings at work, and he knew that a fifth meant he would be fired, but he stayed out anyway. He was late this morning and that was it. No more job. Along with no money left in his accounts and a credit card bill which would take a lottery win to pay off.

"Hey handsome. Waiting for me?" She kissed his neck and grabbed his hand. "Let's get out of this dive."

Mark didn't look at Steve as he followed her out.

* * *

Jasmine propped her foot on the bench and tightened her shoelace. This was the second morning of her new plan to run before work every day. It wasn't as thrilling as yesterday had been. The excitement of doing something good for herself was replaced today with aching calves and sore feet. Maybe an hour was too much to start off with. Didn't the experts say you should start off slow and build up? Forty-five minutes was probably a better goal.

Or thirty, she thought as she panted up the hill. Then she would have time to shower and grab a coffee on the way to work.

* * *

Jack stared down into the grocery cart. Steak, carrots, wheat bread, spicy mustard, and onions. There was something else. He tried to picture the list he had left on his kitchen table. Maybe if he walked up and down a few aisles he would remember.

Coffee filters and butter. Those had been on the list. But the bottle of Jack Daniel's and the case of chardonnay had not.

* * *

The blue capsules were better than beer and The Madam seemed to have an endless supply. Mark abandoned his feeble attempts at finding work and simply spent every day sitting on the porch waiting for her silver Mercedes to appear. He quit worrying about his debt, and things were better since he'd told her he lost his job. She paid for their meals and cover charges now. And he really was drinking less now that he had the pills.

His rent was overdue and his phone had been shut off, but hey, what's a guy to do? Maybe she would float him a loan. He just had to figure out how to ask her.

* * *

"What are you doing here?" Jasmine would have laughed at the sight of Mrs. S in spandex tights and running shoes, but the creepy aspect of the woman showing up unannounced to jog was overwhelming.

"I thought I would join you on your run, dear. I know how eager you are to lose weight." Mrs. S jogged in place as she spoke. She looked at Jasmine's feet with a frown, as if standing still were a crime.

Jasmine considered telling the old woman she had already run her sixty minutes. But Mrs. S had an uncanny way of seeing through her lies.

"Let's go," was all she could think of in reply and she set off down the path at twice her normal pace. She was young. She would outrun her unwanted partner.

* * *

"You aren't going to believe what happened!" Essie burst into his house without knocking. When had she become so familiar? Even Peter rang the bell and they had been friends since college.

Jack slid his mug into the sink. The brown liquid could pass for the last of a morning cup of coffee. He didn't want Essie to catch him drinking this early. After he checked his investments this morning—falling again—he'd needed a little nip to ease the pain.

"What happened?" He didn't think he was actually meant to guess.

"I got robbed! Right in front of the mini-mart."

"Robbed? How? Did they snatch your purse?" He looked for the brown leather near-suitcase proportion bag she usually toted. He wouldn't mind if she had to replace it. With something a bit more classy.

"At knifepoint. He grabbed me, just like in the movies. I thought he was going to say 'your money or your life' but he didn't. He said 'open the car' and took my purse."

Essie spoke rapidly and her chest heaved up and down with each gasped sentence. Yet her blue eyes flashed not with fear, but as if the robbery excited her.

"Did you call the police?"

"The clerk did. She was watching the whole thing." Essie paced the kitchen. "It's not safe out there. Jack, will you help me buy a gun? I don't know anything about them."

A gun? Why did she think he knew anything about guns? He imagined Essie with a six shooter, blowing away some innocent bystander.

"I don't think that's a good idea. This was just one of those

114

things, you know? Bad timing. I'm sure it won't happen again."

Essie stopped marching back and forth and faced him. "That's easy for you to say, safe here in your mansion. You don't know how scared I was." Her eyes turned down, filling with tears. She shook her head rapidly and sobbed. Then she flung herself against him and cried into his chest.

The transformation was unlike anything Jack had ever witnessed. As if stage instructions were being called out in an improvisational theater. Now be scared, now be excited, now be misunderstood.

* * *

"Have you thought about joining a gym?"

Mrs. S wasn't even panting. Jasmine realized her plan to smoke out the lady wasn't going to work. How could someone that old keep up a steady pace of criticism and run at the same time?

"When would I work out at a gym?" Jasmine gasped out her reply and looked ahead. The top of the hill looked miles away. She would never make it.

"Maybe a different job? Something outdoors? It's not good to be sitting at a desk all day long."

"Cramp." Jasmine stopped and dipped her head to her knees. She had to come up with a way to get rid of Mrs. S.

* * *

"You don't look so good."

Mark thought she spoke out of concern. Maybe she would fix him up with something that could make him forget about the eviction notice he had been served with today.

"I think you'll stay home tonight. They'll throw us out of Lagintos with you looking like this."

"No problem," he answered. Hadn't he been telling her they should stay in some nights? He was exhausted from all this partying, though it didn't seem to slow her down a bit.

"I'll call you."

She was out the door before he could protest. He hadn't meant that he wanted to stay home alone.

The least she could have done was leave him some of the capsules.

* * *

Jack had never seen a woman so angry. Certainly Karen had never said the kind of things Essie shot at him, like bullets from a gun.

The gun.

That stupid gun. He should have left the whole thing alone. None of his business, really. If the woman wanted a gun— needed a gun—to feel safe, so be it.

But she couldn't really expect him to take part in something he disagreed with from the start.

He went to the kitchen, pulled a mug from the cupboard and filled it with bourbon. It was only as he returned to the family room that he noticed her purse—the replacement every bit as huge and ugly as the stolen bag—sitting on the edge of the couch.

Damn. She had stormed out without it. Frankly he hoped he would never see her again and now she would need her bag.

"You call yourself a man?" she had screamed. "A liquored up has-been. You drank Karen's life away and now you want to drink mine away too."

The more she yelled, the more he drank. Silently.

Until she brought up the subject of his investments.

"Some kind of genius you are. I've tripled my stocks this year. Me, a stupid woman with no financial sense. That's what you think of me, isn't it? Well, the joke's on you, Mr. I'm-the-only-one-who-knows-what's-best-for-you. Wasn't Clone Optics your last shot at it? Belly up, that's what it's called. What would Karen have thought about that? Losing her life savings. Nothing left for her kids to inherit."

He couldn't keep quiet.

"You leave Karen out of this. It has nothing to do with her. This is about you. Your irrational fears."

"The only thing irrational about me is the fact that I've stayed around a loser like you for so long."

That was when he threw the empty glass across the room and Essie stomped out the door.

* * *

"Hey Mom. How are you?"

117

"Who is this?"

Did her mother really say that?

"It's me, Mom. Jaz. We haven't talked in a long time. I got a promotion and I thought we could go out and celebrate."

"What are you talking about? I don't even live in the same state. We can't just grab a bite."

"That's what I'm saying, Mom. I want you to come visit."

"Fly out there? What would I do all day?"

"I have some vacation time coming. We could see the sights."

"Look honey. I'm glad you got what you wanted, but I'm in the middle of something. Can we talk about this some other time?"

Click.

She never got what she really wanted.

* * *

Jack picked up the purse. He would mail it to her, that's what he would do. Right now and then send her a text telling her she could expect it. Overnight delivery and no excuse for her to ever set foot in his house again.

This handbag was even bigger and bulkier than the other one. He looked inside for a wallet. He would get her address off her driver's license.

The smooth barrel of a revolver was unmistakable and he yanked his hand out in shock.

She had the gun already.

Jack started to shake, picturing her anger, her rapidly changing mood, her excitement at the thought of defending herself. He was damn lucky she hadn't pulled out the gun and shot him. The ultimate way to win an argument.

This meant he couldn't mail the purse to her. Not with a weapon inside it.

He needed a drink. He took the glass and the bottle out to the deck and sat on the Adirondack chair Karen had refinished. It was one of the last things she had done before she got sick.

He stayed out there until the bottle was empty.

* * *

"Have another." The Madam held out a blue capsule.

Mark focused on her palm, the pill lying against the soft, pink flesh. It reminded him of something but he couldn't clear his thoughts enough to remember.

Try, try, try to think. It's important. You need to remember. Was it his mother? Had she handed him something once?

His phone buzzed. He focused on the words but they wouldn't sit still. Steve. It was a text from Steve.

Maybe a shower would help.

She was here again. Had she been gone?

"I don't think I need—"

"Of course you don't think. You never think, do you? If you thought, you would have a job and a place to live. You wouldn't be dependent on an old woman to support you."

The Madam had not taken kindly to his suggestion she might

loan him some money.

He closed his eyes and reached for the pill, then opened them again when his hand didn't meet up with anything.

Her palm was closed and pressed against her chest. Those breasts he had taken such pleasure in…before…before…before what? He squinted and tried to see her. Who was she anyway?

Now her hand was empty and she laughed. Had he swallowed the pill or had she put it in her own mouth? He remembered water, a parched mouth and water. He must have taken the pill.

"The blue is true but the yellow is mellow."

Now she held out another pill. A yellow tablet. He hadn't seen this one before. He blinked and opened his mouth, his tongue thrust forward like a communicant waiting for the holy wafer.

"The yellow is so mellow but the red will make you dead."

He tried to think, tried and tried. If he couldn't move how could he take the red pill? Did he want to be dead? Maybe. Hadn't he wanted to kill himself before? He had been so down and out and now things were much worse than that. Nothing. He really had nothing.

He couldn't even turn toward her, couldn't part his lips. But he felt, saw, sensed her pushing the pill into his mouth, her finger moving gently—she always had such a gentle touch—far enough back so that he gagged a bit, but swallowed.

His phone. It was buzzing again, but he couldn't find it.

"The mouth is prime but the vein makes time."

What the hell did that mean? Had she said that or was his

phone playing a song?

Mark never felt the tightening of the rubber or the sting of the injection.

This feels good. Great, I'm going somewhere. I don't have to worry about that buzzing. Or that other thing, what was it? Doesn't matter. Doesn't matter at all.

* * *

"There's a better route we can take."

Great, not only had Mrs. S continued to show up every morning, but now she was going to boss Jasmine around about this too.

"I'm just thinking about you, dear. That hill, you might not be ready for it yet."

Jasmine glanced at the woman. It was true, really. When had Mrs. S done anything other than be nice? She did seem to always be thinking of Jasmine and how to make things better. Sometimes they might backfire—look at all the weight she had gained from those delicious lunches—but could she really fault the woman for fixing her a meal?

Mrs. S was not like her mother. Mrs. S always had time for her. Every single day.

"Sure. I'll try a new route."

Jasmine followed on Mrs. S's quick heels as they wound through the park and out the other side. Pretty soon they were on the edge of the district, running along the sidewalk in front of an area of town Jasmine usually avoided. Visions of muggers and gangs filled her head.

"Do you really think this is a good way to go?"

"Scared? Maybe that'll make you run a bit faster."

Yeah. There was that too. Mrs. S's bitchy side.

They came to a stoplight and Mrs. S veered left and down. Didn't this take them to the river? Now Jasmine was really getting scared. The water was rushing and gray, filled with trash. The trail was no better. Abandoned grocery carts, wadded up bags, broken bottles.

She stopped. "I don't want to go this way."

Mrs. S didn't slow, just called over her shoulder. "Be a good girl and keep running."

The path curved up onto a thick concrete retaining wall which served as the river bank here in the city, keeping the angry water away from the houses and offices. Jasmine hesitated, thinking Mrs. S would stop and turn back now.

The crazy woman didn't, just hopped up onto the edge of the wall and kept running. Not wanting to be left alone, Jasmine scrambled up and tried to catch her.

This was crazy. Everything about Mrs. S was crazy. Why had she thought, even for a moment, that doing what this lady said was a good idea?

The top of the concrete wall was uneven and narrow. Up ahead Mrs. S ran is if she were on the new padded track at the high school. Her skinny legs pumped up and down and Jasmine could swear she was running faster.

Trying to ditch her.

Damned if she was going to let the crazy bitch do that.

Jasmine sped up, keeping her eyes on the wall and placing her feet in spots that were free of debris.

She glanced up every few steps. She was gaining on Mrs. S.

When Jasmine ran into the old lady at full speed, Mrs. S should have been the one knocked off the wall and into the freezing river below.

Sometimes the laws of physics play games. As Jasmine fell she caught sight of the woman's face. Those pale blue eyes, those ears tucked under gray hair, the eyebrows which dipped and curved with each bit of advice.

She heard something. A grating laugh, echoing down the wall, down to the river.

Just before her body hit the water—to be swept miles downstream before it was discovered a week later—the face was replaced. The eyes that stared after her as she fell and fell, helpless and alone, were those of her mother.

* * *

Jack stared at the empty bottle and ran his hand over the smooth armrest of the chair. Karen had been meticulous in her refinishing jobs.

Was there another bottle in the kitchen? He could go and look, but getting up required more energy than he could muster. As he considered his options, sobs took over. Damn alcohol always did make him emotional.

I miss you, Karen. I really miss you. It wasn't supposed to happen this way. I was supposed to take care of you. If I had only quit drinking a few years early. I would have been there. I would have taken you to those hideous chemo appointments. I would have held your hand and kept the light going in your eyes. Instead I wasn't looking. I never saw you give up, but that's what happened, isn't it?

He threw the empty bottle across the patio, but it hit the lawn and failed to give any sort of satisfying crash. He wiped his eyes with the back of his hand and pulled himself up. There was another bottle and he would drink that one too.

When Jack got to the kitchen he was surprised to see an empty on the counter. Had he just drank two bottles of Jack Daniel's? He searched the cabinet but everything was gone. When had that happened? He had restocked the thing just a few days ago.

He was searching for his keys—he wasn't too drunk to drive down to the mini-mart and get another bottle—when he saw Essie's purse. Still sitting on the couch where he had dropped it.

Jack walked over and pulled the gun from the bag. It wasn't the six-shooter he had imagined, but a tiny little semi-automatic. A ladies gun, he supposed. Light weight.

Jack thought about Essie. What a crazy woman. It was her, really. She was the one that made him start drinking again.

Oh, Karen. Can I really blame Essie? Didn't I fail you long before she was in the picture?

Jack felt the same sense of hopelessness he had felt the day Karen died. The day his children looked at him in disgust, his daughter calling him a hopeless pig, his son never saying a word.

The gun felt warm in his hand. With his mind racing and yet

feeling as if his thoughts were in slow motion, Jack put his finger on the trigger and raised the gun to his mouth.

* * *

The smartly uniformed doorman picked up the aqua suitcase and swung it into the trunk of the silver Mercedes. The beautiful woman was checking out today after a long stay. It was his last chance to get one of her generous tips.

"It's sure been nice having you here, Mrs. Sweesidy. You be safe on those roads, there's quite a storm coming."

She smiled at the mispronunciation of her name and handed him a twenty.

People never pronounced her name. It was just too hard on them to say it the way it looked. She never corrected them, although at times she thought if they would just pay attention they would be able to resist her charm.

She slipped into the driver's seat and waved to the doorman. Chris, that was his name. A happy guy, who appreciated her tips but had no need for her expertise.

Greta Suicide gunned the engine and sped off. Her time here had been productive, even if that girl, Jasmine, wasn't really quite ready for her services. She wouldn't try that line of seduction again. San Francisco was her next stop. There was always plenty of work in that town.

LAYERS

A low-hanging branch whipped against his cheek and the rigid leaves struck his eyes, but even momentary blindness didn't stop Matias from running. The path was narrow, but he knew it as well as he knew the lines that ran across the palm of his hand. He didn't slow to rub his eyes—only blinked to clear his vision.

He didn't want his vision cleared. He didn't want to see the milky eyes of Brother Rabbit. The bright life gone—replaced by something so wretched he hadn't been able to keep the tears from spilling down his cheeks.

"You cry like a woman," Grandfather had spit out, snatching the body of the hare and waving it. "Go back to your Grandmother until you are truly ready to become a man."

He was ten years old. Plenty old enough to be a man.

Matias had found Brother Rabbit when he was eight years old. The small hare had been hiding behind a stone at the river. Brother Rabbit had not been afraid, as all other rabbits were. The brown ball of fur had hopped over to Matias, nose wiggling and ears flapping. The boy had picked up the creature and held him close to his chest. Both hearts beat as one. From that day on the rabbit slept curled next to Matias. The two had crawled out of bed each morning to explore the fields. Brother Rabbit nibbled grass and flowers while Matias collected rocks and bugs, his nose as close to the ground as the hare's. When the sun filled them with too much joy to be contained in their slow rambling they would race and jump, moccasined feet and furry paws kicking up to the sky.

Matias broke clear of the forest. Now the trail ran up a steep gully, slippery gravel slowing his run. His lungs pumped and sweat covered him like a spring rain. It wasn't until the boy reached the snow line that he stopped and looked back.

He could see the whole valley from up here, the layers that formed his world. Low gray river, snakelike down the center of the valley, green meadow dotted with the lean-to buildings where his family lived, the dark forest where the men hunted, crowned with the shimmer of granite and snow sharply outlined by the turquoise sky. Each strip of his life met the next with a striking boundary, as if forest could never commune with meadow, or river could not love granite. The rules were hard and fast.

All his life he had watched as the men brought home deer or fox or squirrels or hares. The animals were skinned and the meat salted and dried. When the hunter was successful the families celebrated. The fire would blaze and the sizzle of the roasting flesh would accompany the smells that drifted through the village.

Matias never ate the meat.

"Ah, we will feast tonight," Grandfather would say.

"I can hardly wait," Grandmother would answer.

But the smell meant only one thing to Matias: Death. And the taste in his mouth was that of the blood that had filled it when he was a child.

The blood of his mother.

He was not much more than an infant when his parents had been struck down. No one would tell him the whole story. He didn't know who it was that had delivered the fatal blows to the heads of his parents, who had kicked them and stripped them of their horse and their belongings. These unnamed butchers hadn't noticed or hadn't cared about the child wrapped in the deer skin papoose, holding him close to his mother as the blood poured from her head and face and ears. Blood that covered him, too tightly bound to move away from her and too scared to want anything other than to be close.

Grandfather had found him and carried him back to the village, where Grandmother's tears fell onto him and mixed with the water she used to wash the blood of her daughter from her grandson's face.

Matias shivered as the cold wind blew off the snow. People grew older no matter what. He would become a man just with the passage of time. The sun would rise every morning and the moon would come out each night. He had grown as tall as his grandmother already, without eating flesh.

He stripped away Grandfather's glare. Below it lived Grandmother's warm touch as she brushed the hair from his forehead. When her fingertips touched his skin he felt his mother's touch, the memory as vague as smoke drifting off the cook fire and as clear as the snow covered peaks against the spring sky. Below it his mother's smell—a fragrance unmatched in this world, the combination of spicy pine bark and sweet berries. He dug deeper and found the heartbeat he had shared with her, and then felt it fade and found once more the rhythm he had shared with Brother Rabbit.

Matias stood and faced the world. The expansive layers of trees and water and sky and clouds. The land where he lived and the land where his brothers lived.

"Aaayiii!" He yelled. He filled his lungs. "Aaayiiii!" He waited until the echo died before he turned back to the trail and set off down the mountain. He would be a man, but he would be a man who respected life. He would grow tall and wise, working beside the women. He would walk beside the men and make Grandfather see that the old ways did not have to be the only way. He would stand strong, calling on the gentle spirit of his mother, the bold spirit of his father, and the laughing spirit of Brother Rabbit. He would be different than any man had ever been. The world would be different, but it would be better, not wrong.

He would not kill his Brother.

Armed But Not
Dangerous

It was Thanksgiving day when Aunt Sophie died. Two months later I inherited the gun.

I didn't know you could get a weapon that way—not with all those legal requirements. Licenses and waiting periods and background checks. But there it was, tucked in Great-Aunt Sophie's hope chest amidst the Royal Albert China and the embroidered linens.

It wasn't loose or anything. It was in one of those special boxes, metal, with a key to keep children safe.

I've always wondered about that. Hiding a gun in a locked box. Kids are wily. If they can find the box, they can find the key. If I had children I would wear the key around my neck on a chain long enough to let the cold metal dangle just between my breasts, a secret reminder that I was protected.

Except if your gun is locked away in a box and you have to fumble down inside your bra for the key, how protected are you?

I didn't take the gun out of the box. For all I knew it was

loaded and I was no fool. I'd heard all those news stories about toddlers and wives and houseguests being killed by an unloaded gun. So there the gun stayed, sleeping safely with the linens as it had no doubt done for years, Great-Aunt Sophie being ninety-eight when she passed.

People said I had a lot in common with her. But I didn't like Royal Albert China and I left it in the hope chest too. I did use some of the linens. I think she must have been saving them for her trousseau. Too bad she never married. That's probably why people think we're alike. I will never marry.

Oh, it's not for lack of trying. I went through all that stuff young girls go through. Primping and prepping for dates, studying glossy magazines and taking the so-called psychological tests to check out my compatibility factors. I even went to an astrologer to match my sign with the right man.

You see, I didn't want to be stuck in the wrong marriage. Not like my sister.

Nan was twelve years older than I was and married at nineteen. So I watched the evolution and de-evolution of that relationship. How things started out so romantic, and a mere ten years later she was cheating and he ran off with the kids. Now they both slept with someone else and fought over visitation rights.

The bad news was no one ever got far enough with me to consider leaving as "running off" with anyone. The good news was I was used to living on my own. An old maid already, I had flown past the point of no return. I would never change my ways. I slept in the center of the bed.

But I digress. We were talking about the gun. How it was tucked away. That is, until the night those hoodlums broke into my house. Muffy barking up a storm and me hearing the sound of glass breaking and crawling under the bed. I held the stupid dog tight enough to strangle him before he shut up. (For those animal activist out there, I didn't actually strangle him, it's just a turn of phrase for heaven's sake.) Anyway, that changed my attitude about the gun and the lock and how safe I really was. I even thought about the fact that a husband might have protected me. But I could be wrong about that. Men aren't really like the guys in the movies, are they?

After the police left, giving no reassurance that they would ever pursue the intruders in any way—*these things happen, keep your doors locked*—I knew I had to do something. My doors had been locked. Did I need to board up my windows? I took the box that held the gun out of the hope chest and stared at the weapon.

There were details one might miss at first glance. A scrolling design on the handle, complete with the initials S. M. The smooth wood was marbled, with a carved-out grid of diamonds on the back of the handle—which must keep it from slipping in your hand—but made the gun into a piece of artwork. Good thing because my hand would be sweaty when I held the weapon. The metal of the gun gleamed, even after sitting in the box for who knows how long.

S.M. Great-Aunt Sophie's last name was Mason. And as I said, like me, she never married. I wondered about the story behind the gun. A gift? From who? Or whom? I never could get that particular grammatical puzzle firmly pressed into my mind.

No matter. I needed to protect myself. I would have to practice shooting the gun. Once should be enough, but it couldn't be here. I carried the box to my car and set it on the floor, carefully pointing the muzzle—the part where the bullet comes out on this kind of gun, a hand gun, I knew that much—toward the passenger door. What if it went off when I drove over a bump and shot the innocent person who was driving in the next lane? I pointed the muzzle toward the back. A bullet would go under the seat and have to travel all the way through the rest of the car. I wondered how many layers a bullet could penetrate. There would be lots of damage to my car, but no damage to my engine or an innocent bystander.

I drove outside of town, following the curving Crater Canyon Road to a spot without houses. A dirt track which wound around the edge of a meadow offered me a way to pull off the main road.

I opened the box and the gun stared at me from its foam nest. Fierce. I imagined Aunt Sophie facing off with a group of thugs who threatened her life. In my mind she was dressed in a lace dress and shiny black heels. In reality she had never dressed like that. Worn-out khakis and flannel shirts. She probably carried the gun in her waistband.

I reached into the box and picked up the weapon, careful to keep the killing part pointed away. It was heavier than I expected, the long nose of it tipping downward. I couldn't hold it up with one hand, so I used two.

Didn't guns have some sort of safety switch to keep them

from going off? I searched the body part of the weapon. Trigger, I knew that much. There was a little lever, but which way was on and which way was off? I carefully pushed it up. It made sense that it had been put away with the safety on.

For that matter wouldn't it have been put away without any ammunition? My hands began to tremble and I set the gun on the seat and searched the box.

Just a foam liner cut out to hold the weapon. I pushed on it and my finger sank to the bottom of the metal box without resistance. No hidden bullets.

Stop it. Just do it.

I picked up the gun and got out. How far would it shoot? Didn't assassins hide in the windows of apartment buildings and shoot down to the street? I looked across the meadow.

This area wasn't totally unpopulated. What if there was a cottage hidden in those trees?

I looked up. If I shot at the clouds the bullet had to come down somewhere.

I walked to a flat rock ten feet ahead. The rock afforded me twelve inches of height and I pointed the gun down into the meadow. At this trajectory it would go into the dirt.

I hoped.

My finger trembled as I gave the trigger a tiny press. Nothing. I would have to press harder.

Licking my lips I told myself I could do this.

Just then a covey of quail burst from the edge of the meadow and raced in front of me. The proud male with his conquistador feather, followed by the hens and chicks, little fuzzy blobs racing under their mother's feet.

I certainly didn't want to kill any birds.

I turned to the right and pointed the gun. This time I pulled with all my might and closed my eyes.

Nothing.

Heart pounding, I walked back to the car. I wouldn't be shooting anything today.

The next day I decided I would take a class. But who taught them? The sheriff's department? I pulled out the yellow pages. This wasn't a 9-1-1 call.

"Plumqua County Sheriff's Department, Nancy speaking."

"Umm . . . I want to find out about a class. For guns?" I slammed down the phone. What if it wasn't legal to have Aunt Sophie's gun at all? I assumed that it being in the hope chest meant someone knew it was there. But who? The lawyer surely didn't go through all of her things.

I was probably supposed to register it. Now I was not only a gun owner, but a criminal.

What if Nancy, Plumqua County phone-answerer, traced my call? My phone number and address had probably popped up on a screen the minute she picked up the phone.

Better to be honest. That's what I had learned in life. Well, to a point, honesty was the best policy. Generally speaking. Although as I dialed again I reflected on all the times honesty had screwed me.

Like with relatives. When you told them what you observed, how they were messing things up, they never really saw it like you did. My sister accused me of being a pompous bitch without a clue when I suggested that her moving out on her family wasn't the best idea. She didn't consider my advice helpful.

The men I dated didn't really think the truth was all that important either. When I made tiny—really, teeny, tiny—suggestions about things that would make the date more enjoyable, their faces grew stiff. One fellow, I think his name was Jeff, got up and walked out of the restaurant without another word.

"Plumqua County Sheriff's Department, Nancy speaking."

She was consistent.

"Sorry. I think we got cut off. What I wanted to ask, you see, I inherited a gun and . . . do I need to do something? Is there a class or something?"

"Depends on the gun. Look on our website. All the regulations are listed."

"I'm not so big on computers. Is there a booklet?"

There was. After she took my name and address and credit card number.

Then Nancy, in her purely business voice, told me where to call for classes.

The class had a waiting list. Unless I wanted to go to a hunter training class, but the kind man who answered the phone at the shooting range said he thought I would be much happier in the "Women Warriors" class.

Did I have to dress in a super-hero costume?

I had him put my name on the list and after I once again

gave my credit card number, I was set. Now I just had to wait five weeks and hope the intruders didn't come back before I learned how to protect myself.

I thought about bars on the windows, moving, and shooting the gun. I thought about blood and bodies exploding and flesh splattering my walls. I thought about someone holding a gun to my face, to my head, and shooting me in the knee. I thought about all this while I didn't sleep a wink for the next thirty-five nights. I even thought about Jeff and Carlton and Gerald and all the other men I had dated. Carlton would have been the most protection. He was big and moved fast, trained at a gym or something. He would have protected me.

Finally the day of the class arrived. I had studied the map to see where I was going and I was surprised to see the range was located near the tiny county airport. I didn't see how a shooting range could be near an airport. Wouldn't there be a chance of a bad shot piercing an airplane? My hands were sweaty at the thought that I would be in close proximity to other people. Women who dreamed of being warriors and probably knew everything about guns already. Tattoos. Black hair. Leather studded vests.

When I found 2365 East Runway Drive, I was surprised to see an industrial park. A blazing red and yellow sign, "GUNS", told me I was in the right place, but it was simply a glass-fronted building with thick iron bars on the windows. I sat in the car and stared at the sign. Was this the right thing to do?

Voices interrupted my doubtful thoughts.

"Oh Betty! What did you say?"

The voices came from two women walking toward the door of Plumqua Shooting Center. I watched them in my mirror.

"I told him I wasn't coming back," Betty's companion answered.

They were wearing blue denim pants and sweatshirts. One had gray hair, the other dyed mahogany. Both a little on the plump side.

No black leather, no studs and no tattoos.

I could do this.

"Hello. Welcome to Women Warriors. I'm Adele. Did you bring your own weapon?"

The young woman who greeted me smiled without using her lips. She looked over my shoulder.

"Uh . . . yes." I held up the case.

"Let's just bring it over here. We don't allow any ammo in the classroom."

I followed her to the counter. I watched as she lifted Great-Aunt Sophie's gun, flipped a little lever and pulled out the round part on the side. I recognized the slots for bullets from the old time cowboy movies I loved to watch. Adele spun the bullet holder part and pushed it back into place. She put the gun back into its case and snapped it shut. There hadn't been any bullets.

"Great. You can take this in and find a seat."

The small room was filling fast. Tables and chairs were crammed together, all facing a whiteboard. Boxes were stacked along the walls, making the one aisle on the side of the room a tight squeeze. Two guns and a stack of papers sat on the table at each spot. I squeezed past the women I had seen in the parking lot and took a place in the back row, just as a slim woman with curly black hair walked to the front of the room.

"Hi. I'm Charlene and I am one of your teachers today. We also have Adele with us, you probably met her on your way in. Kate and Sharon will be here later, when we go out on the range."

I liked Charlene. She started at exactly ten o'clock, as advertised. Even if she dressed a little slutty.

"You should have two weapons in front of you, as well as any you brought with you. There is a handout and we will follow it for this class. A sign-in sheet is going around the room. Please check your information for accuracy. Names matter. Spelling, middle name, everything. This information must match exactly for your weapon registration. If you are planning on getting a CCW this is critical. Your application will not go through with any irregularities. If you go by Meg but your name is Margaret, pick the one that is on your official ID. Such as your driver's license."

As Charlene's lecture continued I pondered the gaps in my vocabulary: CCW? caliber? semi-automatic? We were interrupted when the door opened and two ladies—well, hardly more than girls—bounced in.

"Hi! Sorry we're late. We got lost." The blonde wearing a snug t-shirt looked around the room for an empty chair. Make that snug and made of thin fabric. This one wanted us to see the stitching in her tiny bra. The other girl, a brunette in a striped button up, smiled nervously.

"There's a seat up here and one in the back." Charlene waved toward the empty chairs.

Tight-shirt scowled, then smiled, flashing very white teeth. "We kinda wanna sit together."

So much for starting on time. Now everyone shifted, moved purses, weapons, and lunch bags so that the two infants could sit together.

Next to me.

"I'm Rachel," Blondie announced. She reached for the large canvas purse she had hung on the back of her chair. "These are my guns."

With that she dumped the contents of the bag on the table. Guns poured out as Charlene rushed down the tiny side aisle.

The blast deafened me. Screams filled the room. My scream was the loudest. I felt the wind of the bullet as it whistled past my shoulder. I heard the wall crunch under the impact.

Charlene didn't waste any time. She literally leaped over the stack of boxes in her way and pushed her body between Rachel and the weapons.

"We're okay. Everything is okay," she spoke in a commanding voice. "Don't move."

Nobody moved. A few of us sobbed. I was shaking so hard my throat closed and breathing was a thing of the past.

Charlene worked like the cops in that series, the one in its tenth straight season. All business in spite of her high heels and tight knit tank top. She removed the guns from the room, opened the window for some ventilation, asked anyone if they needed the bathroom or some tea and then suggested we get started.

"I need..." My throat was still cramped. "I'm not going to..."

Charlene glanced at Adele and motioned with her head. Adele rushed to me.

"Let me help you." She grabbed hold of my arm and nearly carried me from the room.

My knees were shaking so hard I couldn't stand. As soon as we were outside the classroom I sank to the floor.

"That...I almost died."

"It was an unfortunate accident. Charlene is going to talk about safety first thing. How about we get you some water so you don't miss any of her lecture?"

I shook my head and rolled to my knees, pushing myself up enough to grab onto the shelf and stand.

"I'm going home." I started toward the door, then stopped. "Can you get my purse for me?"

"It's going to be okay, really it is. I think if you go back in and listen you'll be fine." Adele wouldn't give up.

"I really want to go. Will you please bring me my purse."

My message finally got through to her. Maybe it was because I had raised my volume and there was an edge of hysteria in my tone. Adele slipped into the classroom and returned with my purse and the metal case that held Aunt Sophie's gun.

I shook my head and reached for the purse. "I don't want it. You keep it."

"We can't do that. How about I take it out to the car for you." Adele must have decided she needed to see me well on my way before I decided to sue the shop for incompetence.

Driving home, the unloaded pistol tucked into the locked case which now rode in the trunk—Adele had said this was the law about how to carry a weapon in your car—I thought about what came next.

I was scared. Scared of robbers and guns and foolish young women. I needed a solution.

A whole list burned through my head. Move, install an expensive alarm system, go back to the warrior class and learn to use the gun, put iron bars on my windows.

Get married. Let one of those big guys move in.

None of those fixes worked for me.

When I got home Muffy was overjoyed at my return. He bounced around the kitchen while I made myself some tea and jumped into my lap as soon as I sat.

What came next was I put the gun back into the hope chest. And then I went to the animal shelter to look at dogs.

Big, growling, ferocious, dogs with a loud bark. Who got along with little yappers, like Muffy.

Aunt Sophie and I could be alike in so many ways, but I would not be armed. Not today, anyway.

I HEART YOU

Jeff Parker wanted to leave Annie Sandra Parker. She made him miserable.

"Can't you ever put the lid on the jar tight? Look at this mess." Annie Sandra stood in front of the refrigerator, a hydrogen bomb of mayonnaise at her feet.

"Sorry," he mumbled, grabbing a roll of paper towels.

His wife was never to be called Annie or Ann. He had tried when he first met her—*Annie Sandra* stuck on the back of his tongue—but she had corrected him. Her parents had given her the name and they didn't ever expect any variations on that particular theme.

"Now I'll have to eat fast food again because I can't make a tuna sandwich. You know I hate buying my lunch." His wife stomped off, leaving him with a greasy floor.

He was late for work.

"Parker, where the hell were you?" Charles Graham shook his fist and slammed a folder onto the center of Jeff's desk. "Consider this a warning. I want this file to me by ten. With no damn spelling errors. You have a computer and a secretary, for

Christ's sake. Use the spell check."

Jeff sat down at his desk and opened the folder. Twenty minutes later he took the work out to his secretary.

Beth held the folder with two fingers, as if he had just picked it up off the bathroom floor. "Mr. Parker, you have to give me more time. I can't just drop everything because you missed a deadline. I have duties, you know."

Jeff glanced at his watch. Nine forty-five. What other duties did Beth have? She was his secretary, wasn't she? Had he missed the memo that said she was in charge of him?

At five minutes after ten, just as Jeff finished printing off the final copy of a double spell-checked report, his cell rang.

Ignore it. No time. Get the file to Mr. Graham.

It rang again after Mr. Graham had chewed him out for the five minute delay.

Stewart. It might be nice to hear a friendly voice. Jeff stepped into the break room and answered.

"Hey Dude? Did you forget about us last night? Where were you?" Stewart's voice was not so friendly. "Do you know how picky these guys are? Not just anyone gets an invite. I vouched for you, you no-show, and now I am on the shit list."

Poker Group. He had forgotten. Stewart wasn't in the mood for any excuses.

"Whatever. Don't bother asking me for any favors."

Click.

Beth was filing her nails when he returned to his office.

Jeff needed to quit this job. He spent the afternoon working on his letter of resignation.

At 5:00 he deleted it. After he ran spellcheck.

Jeff stopped at the gym on his way home. Bob, the personal trainer he had been working with, was waiting. Jeff glanced at the clock. He wasn't late. Not this time. Why did Bob seem so impatient?

"Let's get started."

"Uh…" Jeff needed to change and put his bag away. He looked down at his suit and leather shoes.

"Fine. Just hurry up."

Was the clock wrong? As Jeff hurried into the locker room he pulled out his phone. Five forty-five. He was fifteen minutes early. What was Bob's deal?

Bob must have taken a hit in the stock market or broken up with his girlfriend or dented his BMW, because he worked Jeff with words that bore the lash of a Viking ship captain.

"Put some muscle into it. You've been at this long enough. No hesitation. What are you afraid of?"

Jeff panted and pushed off for one more triple-plank-three-way-crunch, then collapsed onto the floor.

"We're done." Bob turned and walked away.

Jeff rolled over and looked at the clock. Six ten. What the heck? He'd paid for an hour.

On his way out he stopped at the front counter.

"I would like to cancel my appointments with Bob, the trainer."

Megan, one of the peppy front desk workers, tapped away on the computer. "You signed a contract. Twenty sessions."

"How many do I have left?"

"Fifteen. There are no refunds. Did you want to reschedule instead?"

Jeff closed his eyes and pictured himself confronting Bob. Pushing him in the chest and shouting *I pay you, damn it*. Then he pictured Bob's fist meeting his jaw.

"Okay. How does Thursday look?"

Get mayonnaise. Milk, bread, and fruit too.

The text from Annie Sandra buzzed as Jeff pulled into the driveway. With a sigh, he shifted into reverse and headed to the market. Sixty seconds later the phone chimed again.

He punched accept, assuming it was his wife making sure he saw the text.

"Hi Sweetheart. How's my boy?"

His mother. He should have looked at the screen before he answered the call.

"Fine, Mom."

"I haven't heard from you in such a long time. I heard from your brother. He calls twice a week, sometimes more."

Of course he did. Paul was the good son.

"Did he call you too? With his news?" She bubbled with impatience.

"No." Short responses worked best with his mother because she never let more than two words pass before she interrupted.

"He's a VP now. That means Vice President. He got a promotion." His mother gushed, but under that warm layer the casserole was still frozen. Cold with accusations about Jeff's lack of success. "He has to move to Portland."

Jeff waited. An announcement like his brother leaving the area was certain to be followed by—

"When are you going to get a promotion?"

There it was.

"You should look for a different job. Maybe something in Olympia."

Closer to her, of course. Why she wanted her deficient son near her was a mystery to him.

"Mom, it would be hard to find a job like mine in Olympia. Even tougher to get a promotion if I changed jobs."

"With your brother leaving I'll be on my own. If you had just trained for technology instead of that sales stuff you wouldn't have any trouble finding a job here."

Like your brother, Jeff heard.

"I guess I'll have to move into one of those facilities if I don't want to die alone."

He tuned out the rest of her rambling as he drove to the market.

"I've got to go, Mom. I'm at the store."

"Fine. But think about it. You're not too old for something else."

When Jeff entered the store he was greeted with the sight of shiny heart balloons and a kiosk of red velvet boxes.

Valentine's Day.

He pictured Annie Sandra at home, arms crossed over her chest because she had no mayonnaise and no invitation to a romantic dinner. The tradition she insisted on every year.

Jeff shrugged. At least he had a second chance now. He would grab steaks and potatoes, the cheese she loved, and a bottle of champagne. The requisite card and flowers would save him.

He wasn't alone in the greeting card aisle. Four men stood in front of the cards squinting and scowling and picking up cards, only to return them to the rack and try another.

It was never easy to pick out a card for Annie Sandra. Too cutesy and her fake smile would be plastered to her face for the rest of the week. They didn't seem to share a sense of humor—things he thought were a hoot she found insulting or crude—so a funny card was out.

He picked up a card with a pastel drawing of a couple in silhouette, the pink and orange sky behind them suggested a sunset rendezvous.

Two birds in flight
follow a path of uncertainty
only to dance on the wind.
We alight on the same branch, my love.
The mighty oak does not sway in the breeze
as our two spirits perch side by side.
I ♥ you

What did this even mean?

His phone buzzed. *Did you get my text?*

He tapped the keyboard. *On my way. Bringing a surprise with me. Don't cook.*

He had felt romantic about Annie Sandra in the beginning. And she had stuck with him, hadn't she? Sure she complained, but he deserved it. He didn't put the lid on tight, didn't put the toilet seat down, didn't get a promotion, didn't look for a job in a town that would give them better housing options. And while his job was a dead end, his boss was an idiot, and his secretary a snotty little thing, Annie Sandra kept her job and contributed more than half their income. Look at all those other wives who stayed at home and had children and forced their husbands to work eighty-hour weeks. Annie Sandra stuck it out.

And sticking with him apparently wasn't easy. Even his trainer—someone he paid to help—had given up on him, his best friend had basically booted him out of the group before he ever joined, and his mother would never be satisfied.

Annie Sandra had accepted his proposal, married him, stayed with him, and tried to make their life smooth. That's all it was, her endless nagging and complaining and scowling and making him sleep on the couch—polishing their relationship. He should be grateful. This card did reflect how he felt about her. Kind of, anyway. And he didn't really have time to read a bunch more.

Jeff tossed the card in the grocery basket and hurried toward the candy aisle. He would get flowers *and* chocolates for his wife.

"Steak? I already ate. It's after seven." Annie Sandra looked at the flowers Jeff held out, but didn't reach for them. "These will need a vase."

He nodded and moved toward the kitchen. He set the bags on the counter and the flowers in the sink. Pulling out the red velvet box, he turned back to his wife.

"Here's dessert."

She glanced up from her book. "Not now, I'm off sugar. Just leave it and I'll take it to work tomorrow."

Jeff walked back to the kitchen. He found a vase for the flowers and unpacked the groceries.

Mother had it wrong. You can be surrounded by people and still be all alone.

He unwrapped one of the steaks and smothered it with BBQ sauce. Then he opened the red velvet box and helped himself to seven chocolates, one right after the other.

SEPARATE VACATIONS

There is such a thing as too much togetherness. Kristina had discovered that fact soon after her honeymoon. A trip to Tahiti with every minute scheduled. At the time snorkeling and kayaking and hiking and taking a dance class and a cooking class and a watercolor class were all part of the adventure.

"How about we just lay on the beach tomorrow?" She rolled over and kissed her brand new husband's ear. The stars in her eyes were so bright for Thomas that even sheer exhaustion hadn't stopped her from jumping into all his activities with two excited feet. But a break would be nice.

"Oh, Hon. We only have three more days here. Dive class today." He threw back the thin sheet that covered them and jumped out of bed. "In fact, if we don't get a move on we're going to be late."

After that it was kiteboards and a fishing trip. She never did get to slather herself with sunscreen and listen to the birds and the soft slap of the waves.

Kristina loved Thomas, she really did. He was a dream

husband; cooking, cleaning, paying the bills. Not like her best friend Gloria's husband, who had never touched the dish soap bottle or Elizabeth's partner who threw up his hands in defense when *he* spent their rent money on a new bike.

Not only was Thomas energetic and responsible, he was romantic. He brought bouquets of her favorite purple iris or yellow roses for no special reason. Not for an anniversary or to apologize or get her in the mood. Just because he loved her.

There was such a thing as too much romance.

Last year, when they were in Vegas, she had made the excuse that she needed a spa day and done her best to send him off to the blackjack table.

"Sounds good. What time should we schedule our massages?"

Not exactly what she had imagined, but massages were quiet by nature, so it couldn't be too bad, could it? "Two o'clock?"

When they arrived at the spa Thomas waved at the hall that led to the massage rooms.

"Can you move two tables into one room? We want this to be romantic."

"Uh..." The two masseurs looked at each other and shrugged. "Okay. Give us a minute."

"Really, Thomas? Why make them go to so much work?" Kristina had rubbed his arm, hoping he would see reason.

"Those tables are portable. It's not that much trouble." And when they had gone to the massage room, crowded now with two tables, He pulled out a CD.

"Hey, how about you play this instead of that airy stuff? This is what I can really relax to."

Soft country. That's what her husband called it. Kristina had sighed, rolled her eyes at the therapist and shrugged.

Thomas wasn't finished. Flowers and chocolates delivered to her right there in the spa. She felt like a total glutton, embarrassment replaced flattery as she hauled the stash up to their room.

"Oooo. Someone has a special event," cooed the two old women who shared the elevator. "Anniversary?"

Kristina forced a smile and looked away.

She wanted some distance. Just a few feet. Just for a minute.

For their one year anniversary it had been Europe. Six countries in fourteen days. Her memory was of train stations and castles, but for the life of her she couldn't remember which museum had the wonderful Egyptian display and which was so cold she couldn't take her hands out of her pockets or see much because of the scarf wrapped around her face. England, France, Spain, Italy, Ireland, and one more. Damn, she couldn't remember the sixth country.

Year two was the Hawaiian tour. Thomas had just been promoted at work and he surprised her with a package deal. She hoped the pace would be slower, but no such luck.

"Okay, let's take a look at our schedule." The plane hadn't even left the airport and Thomas had his iPad out and was tapping away. "Helicopter tour on Monday, surf lessons on Tuesday, there's a full day bus tour on Wednesday so we can't add anything on that day, but on Thursday we can sail. I hope I didn't make a mistake signing with a tour. They don't leave us much of our own time."

By year three, Kristina had a plan. She would choose a vacation her husband would hate. Then he would say "You go and I'll stay. No problem."

Thomas had a severe allergy to equine dander. She picked a dude ranch in Montana. With a three day cattle drive. She would be on the horse all day and camping at night. She thought she had convinced him to let her go alone with her tirade of excuses —it was a dream of hers since childhood and it was too good to pass up, such a deal, Gloria had been there and recommended it, it was only offered in June, during his busy time, close of the fiscal year and all, and she would miss him terribly but she really didn't see any other way than to go it alone.

Two days after she made her reservation Thomas burst her bubble. Make that shot down her dirigible in an explosion of flames that rocked the house.

"Good news! They have wagons. I'm signed on as cook's assistant. I won't have to touch a horse at all." He hadn't noticed she didn't return his all enveloping hug.

She signed up for a trip to Paris with a well known fashion designer. Women would sew, buy fabric, and visit the famous "Little Black Dress" shop in the Palais Royal. They all shared rooms. Fashion field trips every day.

Thomas called her at work. "Hey, Kris. Good news. Husbands go all the time. They hang out together while the ladies do their thing. The evenings are free. You won't have to sleep with some snoring dowager."

"Why don't you just tell him?" Her best friend Gloria bit into the health muffin and wrinkled her nose. "Ug. These are nasty. What did you say was in them?"

"Pumpkin seeds and flax. I have tried, believe me I have tried. Last year I used a migraine to get out of the cheese tasting tour and I even stuck my finger far enough to vomit when we were headed for the puppet museum. I spent the next four hours in bed with Thomas stroking my head and heating chicken soup in the microwave. Spooning it into my mouth." The soup had been so salty and her failure so extreme that she had vomited again. Authentically.

"Tell him." Gloria leaned forward and exaggerated every word, as if speaking to a small child. "Thomas-I-don't-want-to-do-so-many-things-when-we-are-on-vacation. I want to sit and watch the sunset. The sunrise. The waves fall on the sand. I want two hours each day by myself."

Kristina shook her head. "I tried that too. He cried, Gloria. Actual tears and sobs. Then he asked me if I was having an affair."

She came up with an infallible plan. Six long weeks touring Peru with a quick jaunt to the Galapagos. There was no way Thomas would take that much time off. No one could be gone that long and expect to keep their job, especially someone who loved his job as much as her husband did. Even if being a consultant allowed him some flexibility and he had worked his way up to a high level position in just five years. There was no way he would go. Kristina—on the other hand—could leave her

157

at-home-editing job whenever she wanted. At the rate she charged missing six weeks would take a bite out of their income, but they were both doing well so it really wouldn't matter. She scheduled their vacation for May, when she knew Thomas would be in the middle of a new contract. He would have to be on the job, making sure everything went right.

She was wrong. Apparently Thomas was high level enough so that he could take six weeks away. As long as he kept in touch. Monitored his underlings with his smart phone.

Kristina rolled her green sweater into a tight spiral and tucked it next to her black jeans and two long sleeve T-shirts. She missed the pre-vacation jitters—that feeling of breathless anticipation she used to get before she and Thomas traveled together—that excitement had been replaced with a dull dread. Not only did she unplug the television and close all the curtains to prepare the house for six weeks of vacancy, she unplugged herself as well. Sleep mode for 42 days was the only way she would manage Thomas in such close proximity—non-stop if he had his way.

Kristina pictured this vacation alone. She would take lots of luggage and pay the fifty dollar baggage fees, filling a huge suitcase with dresses and extra underwear and her favorite coat. Books and watercolor supplies. Five star hotels and plenty of smiling staff to haul her luggage for a thank you and a ten dollar bill.

Not six weeks worth of life in a carry-on.

"Hey, Kris. We can share toothpaste, right? It will save room." Thomas waved two tiny bottles, shampoo and conditioner, in front of her face. "I have these."

"I can't use that shampoo. It makes my hair frizz."

"I'll take a shower right now and use this stuff up. You can fill them with your brand."

She shook her head and snorted, but only in her mind. Thomas wouldn't notice her chin move and he wouldn't hear the slight puff of air leaving her nose. Did he actually think two tablespoons of shampoo would last her six weeks?

Kristina slumped onto the bed, pushing her suitcase to the side. Thomas sang in the shower. Loud. But of course he had a great voice so who was she to complain?

The phone rang.

"Hello?"

"Hello, may I speak to Kristina Brown?"

"Speaking."

"Hi, Miss Brown. This is Andy from the local..."

She put the phone back in it's cradle, not even bothering to respond to the tele-market call. It instantly rang again. The nerve of him for calling back.

"Listen—"

"Is Thomas Brown available?" The caller interrupted Kristina before she could give Andy a scolding.

"Who may I say is calling?"

"Marsha Martin, from Tiger Realty. I'm calling about listing the house."

So much for the Do-Not-Call list. "Please remove our name from your list. We have no intention of selling our house."

Admittedly Kristina slammed the phone down a bit too hard,

her anger at Thomas spilling onto some hard-up realtor resorting to cold calls.

"I reserved us a cab." Thomas set his backpack in the front hall a full two hours before they needed to leave for the airport.

He had bought a pack for her too, but she refused to use it. Good practice for standing her ground, because that was what she was going to do. If she had to travel with him she would make it right. She would speak her mind, plan her time, eat what she wanted and only participate in those activities she had chosen. She would follow Gloria's advice. Two days ago she had set Thomas down and had "the talk." He looked crushed, but that hadn't stopped her.

"Uber is cheaper and I already have one reserved." She smiled and kissed his cheek. "Remember our agreement? I take care of the plans this time."

"Honey, I don't want you to do all the work. This is *our* vacation, remember?"

She did remember. And she remembered his agreement to let her handle things, which seemed to have quickly vanished from his mind. "Which cab did you call? I'll cancel it."

They got to Lima—and the five-star-hotel she had splurged on—without a hitch.

"Let's eat now and then we have some time to look around. A stroll on the boulevard will keep us awake. Have to beat that jet lag!" Kristina kept her voice light and cheery, although she felt a migraine coming on. It had been a very long trip, even without any delays or layovers.

"Sounds like a good idea." Thomas was agreeable. "I'll take the first shower while you unpack."

She had expected him to try to take charge. Even prepared herself for a battle over dinner first or no walk or cocktails instead. Maybe this trip would be different. Kristina opened her suitcase to unroll her single dress. The steam from Thomas's shower should take out all the wrinkles.

The dress wasn't there. Neither was her extra long-sleeve t-shirt or two pairs of her underwear. Her whole suitcase had been unpacked and repacked.

"Oh my God! The airport security robbed me. I didn't even have anything valuable, but they took my clothes."

Thomas sang old rock songs from the shower. He hadn't heard her. He never heard her.

Kristina took inventory. What else had been stolen?

A paperback and her journal. A bottle of conditioner, although the shampoo was still tucked neatly inside a plastic bag and stowed in the bottom pocket.

Why in the world would an airport employee take her dress, her underwear and her shirts and then take the time to repack everything so neatly? Everything re-rolled and color coordinated.

"Heard it through the....la la la."

Thomas.

He had repacked her suitcase.

Heat frothed in her stomach, building up to her throat with a sour acid taste. Her chest spasmed into a tight bowling ball of anger. She would yell at Thomas loud enough to burst through his stupid grapevine song.

Something stopped her. Swallowing hard, she closed her eyes and squeezed the bottle of shampoo. Had he missed it in the hidden pocket or had he simply decided she needed to wash her hair but not condition it?

Not this time. No way. Jumping to her feet, Kristina grabbed her wallet and rushed downstairs. Five star hotels had shops. If she couldn't find a dress there she would head out to the strip down the block.

It took her only thirty minutes to find the perfect small black dress. This really was a nice hotel, with a five star boutique. She added a pair of soft leather pumps and a cobalt rolling suitcase to her bill. She would fill it before the sun set again. Unlike trips Thomas planned, she had included an "adjustment to jet lag" day, which had just morphed into a shopping day.

Thomas was on his phone when she got back to the room.

"That sounds like a decent offer. Go for it." He barely glanced at her as she tucked the new suitcase in the closet and plopped down on the bed. "Hey, listen. I've got to go, we're headed out to dinner. I'll talk to you soon." He slid his phone into the pocket of his very wrinkled jacket. That's what happened when you rolled it tightly into a plastic bag and sucked all the air out—her husband's great space saving trick.

"Working already? They didn't leave you alone for long."

"No...yes...nothing big. Don't worry. I promise it won't impact our time." Thomas stood and straightened his tie. "You ready?"

"Ready? Of course not. My turn to shower." Whatever his office wanted it must have been big to distract him enough so that he never even asked where she had been.

Twenty minutes later she twirled in front of the mirrored closet door and smiled at Thomas who was seated on the edge of the bed clicking through television stations. "Do you like my new dress?"

If only she could have had a video of Thomas's face and the story it told. His need to take control—tight jaw. His realization that he would have to admit to meddling—pressed lips. His anger that she had gone out shopping—raised eyebrow. His decision not to say a word because of a delayed sense of guilt— tongue sneaking out of the corner of his mouth for a split second.

"You look nice." Thomas pushed her hair behind her ear as he kissed the smooth spot on her cheek. "Smell nice too. Excited?"

"Come on, I'm hungry." She pulled him out the door and down the hall.

Kristina smiled as the elevator carried them to the rooftop restaurant. As they rose, her doubts slid down the shaft. She was happy. She forgave her husband for his interference with her packing and she twined her fingers in his. She liked this version of Thomas.

This version—Calm Thomas—stuck around for three days. Kristina had spent all day Tuesday at the shops while he relaxed at the hotel pool. Although she suspected he was working, and not just relaxing because his phone never left his side. Last night they had walked down the avenue—hand in hand again— to a small restaurant recommended by the manager of the hotel: no ambience, he warned, but the best *Choritos a la Chalaca* in Lima.

On Thursday Calm Thomas dimmed.

"I signed us up for a great adventure tomorrow, Kris. A boat ride and this cool truck—like a Mercedes jeep—takes us to this crazy zip-line."

"What? Tomorrow we visit Santo Domingo and I arranged for an authentic dinner with a local family."

"Come on. We have to get away from the city for a day."

"We'll be away from the city on Friday. Tomorrow is our last day here and I want to see the cathedral."

"All cathedrals are the same. Besides, I already paid and it's non-refundable."

Kristina might have enjoyed the boat ride and the zip line, even the crazy vehicle which bounced them through the countryside. But she couldn't. The smile on her husband's face should have made up for the phone call to the local family she made—so sorry, we have to cancel, we'll pay anyway, of course —and the blue skies and breathtaking views were amazing, but Kristina sulked. The real kicker came the next morning, when she started to pack for their move to Trujillo. They were heading north today.

"Hey Baby." Thomas stood behind her and circled his arms around her. "You don't need to pack yet. We're staying here an extra day."

She wrenched herself from his grip and spun around. "What did you do now?"

Hands up, as if to ward off blows, Thomas stepped back. "You wanted to see that church so bad. I booked us another night, that's all. Not the end of the world, I promise."

Maybe not to him, but for Kristina it meant rescheduling their bus, canceling the next hotel—non-refundable at this point in time—and figuring out how this impacted the next few days of her itinerary. If she hadn't built in lots of unscheduled time it would have been a disaster.

"I can't call Marcus. We stood up his family yesterday and that can't be un-done."

"Who the hell is Marcus?"

"The guide, the one I had yesterday. I told you. It was his aunt and uncle who were cooking dinner for us. That was all part of visiting Santo Domingo. Not only that, but I made plans for Trujillo."

"Whatever. I'll see you downstairs. I need coffee." Thomas had stalked away.

In Chiclayo Thomas pulled another fast one.

"Are you ready? The bus leaves in fifteen minutes." Kristina slung her day pack over her shoulder. She was excited about finally seeing Túcume, with it's supposed magic aura and so many pyramids. The website said visitors felt energized and happy after visiting—something she could use right now.

Thomas glanced at his phone. "Umm. Babe. I can't go."

"What?" A soft thump of her heart.

165

"I know I said work wouldn't interfere, but there's a kind of crisis going on, and I need to take care of it."

She stepped forward and kissed his cheek. "Don't worry. It's okay." With a quick pivot, Kristina kept her husband from glimpsing the smile that covered her face.

The day was amazing and Túcume was grand. Walking at her own pace, stopping when she wanted to take a picture, sitting on a boulder for an hour simply to look at the view, everything was perfect. She hoped the crisis at his job would last a few more days.

Calm Thomas disappeared completely. As they traveled back to the south Kristina listened to the him complain about every single thing. No, not everything: just what she planned or did. Listening to his voice was like a high pitch noise that assaulted your eardrums, only slightly relieved by pressing your palms to the side of your head.

"Really, Kristina. Do you have to drink that every morning? It smells disgusting." Thomas didn't care for the new tea she had picked up in Trujillo.

"I think visiting another plaza is a waste of time. I talked to the concierge and there is a balloon trip over the Sacred Valley. I scheduled it for tomorrow."

And when she reminded him of their agreement he got angry.

"Do you have to interrupt me all the time? Can't I even finish a sentence before you disagree with what I want to do? This is my vacation too, you know."

She gave up. It would be his vacation from now on. What was the point in arguing? The crazy thing was he didn't seem to enjoy all the new things he forced on her. His phone buzzed and beeped and rang endlessly.

On Thursday, six days after the disappearance of Calm Thomas, Kristina decided that she would tell her husband they had to go home. The thought of four more weeks of this pinch and pull—Thomas refusing to give up control and she refusing to let go of her resolution that she wouldn't be pushed around—made her stomach burn and her head shimmer with pain.

I'll tell him at lunch, she decided. The airline tickets were in his pack. He had asked for them last night and after ten minutes of argument she slammed the envelope on the tiny desk in the corner of the hotel room. He treated her like a fourteen-year-old, not even trusting her to manage something as simple as the tickets.

"Of course I trust you, Kris. But you didn't even know where the tickets were. You had to search through all those pockets. That's the problem with having more than one suitcase."

She should have known her purchases where stewing deep down in his mission control center. Like a rogue meteor that would likely miss earth, but who knows, we better explode it anyway.

This morning he was out for a run. Something new on this trip—he hadn't asked her to go with him. Happy for a short break each morning she slept in, ordered room service and watched the news. In Spanish, which she found enjoyable, watching the faces of the newscasters, noting raised eyebrows, smiles, shaking heads, waving hands. Put these together with the video footage and she could usually surmise the story with no problem.

Today she used the time to get the tickets out of his backpack. She would call and see what the penalty was for rescheduling their return flight. She unzipped the front pocket where she had watched him tuck the envelope.

Her hand bumped something rigid. It wasn't in the pocket, but behind it. Kristina opened the top of the pack and reached down.

Thomas's iPad? He had insisted that neither of them needed tablets because they had their phones. What else had he smuggled along?

She peered into the pack and pushed a few things around. Shoes, socks, pants, shirts, nothing else that she could see. There wasn't really time to unpack the entire bag, although she wanted to.

A thought came to her. He had been so terrible, right from the beginning. The Calm Thomas phase had been brief, really. When you think about the fact that he had started interfering before they even left the states. Unpacking her bag, taking her things, calling that cab. She quickly slipped the iPad back to its hidden spot. Thomas was hiding something. That must be why he had gone from sweet to sour, not the fact that she was in charge.

"There's something we need to talk about." Kristina set the

spoon down without tasting the cream of asparagus soup.

Thomas slurped a mouthful and nodded for her to continue.

"I want—" An unfamiliar ring tone interrupted her.

"Sorry." Thomas grabbed his phone and looked at the screen. "I have to take this. Work. Sorry, but it's important." He jumped up and hurried out to the lobby.

When had he programed "Baby, What a Big Surprise" into his phone? Who's ring was that?

She stirred the soup without tasting it. Something was off. True to form Thomas wanted to be in charge. But when had he ever been so negative about things? It was impossible for her to complain when he treated her as if she was the most important thing in his world, but his emotional flopping around, snapping at her, rushing off to answer his phone? It wouldn't be hard to tell him she wanted to cut the vacation short if he kept acting like a jerk.

Maybe he was having an affair.

The thought made her laugh, but she choked. Maybe he was. So much romance in that man and she had been denying him his chance to shower her with attention.

In the ten minutes Thomas was away she lost her resolve. If she told him she wanted to go home he would promise to do better, to "lay off" as he always put it. For a few days she would get what she wanted and then things would slide back to the torture of traveling with a man who closed his eyes to her needs. But what if he agreed? Wouldn't that mean he wanted to get back to *her*, whoever she was? The mystery woman?

Maybe she shouldn't even consult him, just change the air

travel tickets and slam them down with the firm directive this trip was over and they were headed home. Or maybe she should just change her ticket, and disappear while he was out running, send him a text message from the airport, leave him to figure out what he wanted to do, each of them in charge of their own destiny.

"Uh, Kristina?" Thomas stood next to the table, clutching his phone.

She snapped out of her daze. "What is it?"

"Bad news, I'm afraid. Things have really fallen apart with the Simpson contract. I have to go home."

"Home?"

"But you can stay. I want you to stay, to do the climb, to see…uh…all those things you have planned."

The "Baby" of the new ring tone must be insisting she couldn't live without him.

"That's what I—" Wait. Why should she tell him now? That she hated this trip, hated the way he smothered her, wanted to go home. Hadn't Thomas just dropped the way out straight into her lap? If he was having an affair she would find out sooner or later, right? Why not take advantage of this bizarre situation?

"Oh, Thomas. Really? Do you really have to go?" Kristina pushed her lips out in a pout to keep the smile suppressed.

"Believe me, Sweetheart, if I could I would pass this off. But it's too big a contract to let Brad screw up. I'm pretty sure I'll have to fire him when I get there and I don't want to do that over the phone. The damage he could do? If I don't protect the files and you know, change his access…all that stuff."

His face was bright red and he was breathing hard. Go for it, buddy. Run off to her. I hope you don't really fire Brad to keep your cover story safe.

"Sit down, Thomas. Finish your lunch at least."

Kristina kept her eyes closed as she stretched her neck, rolling it to the right and rubbing her cheek against the cool pillow. When all the kinks were out she let the filtered sunlight creep into her consciousness and greeted the day. Two days without Thomas and she had never felt better. No headaches, no queasy stomach, no aches and pains at all. Not even after a seven hour hike yesterday.

Today she would leave this hotel. She did love the luxury of 600 count Egyptian cotton sheets but she craved the unknown. Without Thomas she was free to play it by ear. Tomorrow she boarded the bus for the ten days of Matchu Pichu adventure and then it was on to the Galapagos. But there was lots of unscheduled time in between. Unscheduled, unencumbered days that were hers and hers alone. On the original itinerary, carved in stone, they were going to go see canyons and volcanoes in Arequipa, but now? She just might find her isolated beach.

"There are plenty of extra seats, this is a small group, so feel free to spread out. If you sit on the right side of the bus you will see…"

Kristina quit listening to the drone of Margie, the tour guide, and made her way to the rear of the bus. She had expected the tour to be mostly couples, but out of the twenty-seven people only eight were attached. This left a lot of singles. And they all seemed to want to pair up—men and women alike.

No more chatting for me. She slipped into a seat and placed her purse and sweater next to her. For a split second she wished she had a day pack to effectively send the message she wanted to be left alone. To add punch to her communiqué she turned to the window and rested her head, eyes closed.

Someone stopped anyway. She could hear heavy breathing, a gulp, a shift in gait. Eyes tight she waited.

Great. Whoever had considered disturbing her had moved back toward the front of the bus.

Meals were worse. The group was seated at large tables. When Kristina tried to slip off to a table by herself, Jim, a grizzled guy with a comb-over made himself at home.

"Where are you from?"

"Here alone?"

"Mind if I join you?"

"Us single women have to stick together, right?"

She was tired of everyone trying to be her friend. Had she traded Thomas for something worse? Calling up her resolve she put people off. Nice didn't seem to work, so she switch tactics.

"Yes, I am alone because I prefer to travel that way. I think there's room for you over at that table."

Eventually most of the tour group got her message. They paired up nicely and kept out of her way.

Today was the day of the big climb. Kristina was excited and glad she hadn't gone home with Thomas. The weather was clear, just cool enough to be comfortable. She had reviewed the instructions for the new camera—another item that had been on Thomas's taboo list—and was ready to spend the day taking amazing photos.

Margie's voice interrupted the breakfast chatter. "Okay gang. Finish up that coffee and head out front. Today's bus is small, so please move all the way to the back and put your stuff under the seat. We'll be snug, but we can zip up there in no time."

She would have to share. Kristina debated the strategy of waiting to get on last, thus reducing the odds Jim would sit next to her, or getting on first so that she would be sure to have a window seat. She decided the best strategy would be to join the middle of the group.

Everyone had the same idea. All but one of the window seats were taken. This left her with a choice of seat mates, but at the last minute she slipped next to the last window space. Better to have a view and live with who ever sat next to her.

"Is this seat taken?"

Kristina didn't turn from the window, just shrugged. "No." She didn't recognize the voice, but at least it wasn't Jim. She waited for the person to make idle conversation, but all she heard —and felt—was a body settling in next to her. Two minutes later she couldn't resist the temptation to turn and look.

A man. She had never seen him before.

A very handsome man.

He smiled.

"Hi. I'm Kristina. You...I've..." Great, now she was making small talk.

"George. And yes, I'm new to the tour." He offered his hand. A smooth, cool, strong hand.

When the group reached Machu Pitchu, Margie held forth with more instructions. They had already decided which hike—tickets had to be purchased in advance—but there were headsets to pass out and meeting times to be discussed. Kristina told Margie she would be taking the hike alone so she didn't need the guided headsets. She found the ladies room and made her way to the trailhead.

George stood next to the wooden sign—*Bienvenidos* from the *Minsterio del Ambiente*—studying the map. It looked like he had made the decision to go solo as well. Kristina smiled briefly as she moved past him.

"Kristina. I think you might be the type who likes to go it alone, and you can tell me to get lost if you want, but can I join you?" George really did have the sparkliest eyes she had ever seen.

"Why yes. You are right on that account...but I would love it if you joined me." Kristina instantly regretted her words. Why had she said that? She had been planning this day alone ever since Thomas flew home.

Within twenty minutes she knew this would now be the best day of her vacation.

George was nothing like Thomas. He was nothing like anyone she had ever met. There was something about him, a pheromone or a past life or something, but never had Kristina felt so warm with pleasure. She didn't even try to put her finger on what it was—the way he listened, laughed, smiled, held her elbow when they had to perch at the edge of the trail for another group to pass. Maybe it was the calm manner in which he waited for her to set up a photo shot—she wouldn't even describe it as patient because there was absolutely no sense of impatience.

He was real. Even when he asked for something.

"That looks great. You picked the ham, didn't you?" George eyed her lunch.

They were settled on a large stone outcropping, the sun warm enough so that Kristina had removed her sweater and basked like a lizard.

"I did."

"I picked the turkey." He sniffed at his sandwich. "It has pesto, I think. Smells good."

"Hmmm." She took a bite of her ham and swiss. "This is good."

"Can I convince you to go halves?"

"Sure." She handed him half her sandwich.

She liked sharing with George.

She shared a lot with George over the next few days. He had joined the tour late because he had missed his flight from the states. A friend had a crisis and he had stayed to help him move his mother into a retirement home. Kristina was very happy when she discovered he was also booked on the Galapagos tour.

Then she spoke with Thomas.

"Can you come home? You've been gone so long. Maybe we could do those islands some other time. Together."

Had his girlfriend dumped him?

"I miss you too, honey." Hopefully her voice didn't sound as insincere to him as it did to her. "Did you get everything taken care of?"

"How did—oh, you mean Brad and all that. Sure. Most of it anyway."

The goddesses were smiling down on her, because Thomas didn't suggest he fly out to meet her. And she simply refused to consider cutting her trip short.

Marcie was Kristina's favorite Uber driver and she was happy when the quiet woman and her clean Subaru were available for her drive home from the airport. Thomas hadn't returned her calls yesterday and this morning there was only a brief text. *Sorry, can't pick you up. Things still out of control here.* Maybe mystery woman was back in the picture.

"Can you wait?" Kristina asked Marcie. She didn't have a key: one more thing Thomas had insisted she didn't need to bring on their vacation. He had his, so why double up? There was a hide-a-key but it had been months, maybe even a year, since she had used it.

Something was off about the yard. The potted geranium wasn't next to the porch. The ceramic planter with the hidden key was empty. No geranium left at all. What had happened to her plants?

She hoped Thomas had realized she didn't have her key and left the back unlocked. She headed around the side of the house.

A voice interrupted her attempts to open the sticky wooden

gate, always a challenge after a rain storm.

"Excuse me. Can I help you?"

A tall woman in a silk robe stood behind her.

Where had she come from?

"No. It's fine. I'm locked out and just checking 'round back."

"I have to say, you don't look like my idea of a burglar."

Kristina stopped fumbling with the latch and turned to fully face the woman. Who in the world was she? Walking around the neighborhood looking like she just got off a lounger.

"Are you new?"

"Who are you?"

The two women simultaneously shot harsh glares along with their questions.

"I'm Kristina and this is my house. As I said, I've locked myself out."

"Nice try." The tall woman shook her head. "If you leave now, I'll—wait, did you say Kristina? Kristina as in Kristina and Thomas Brown?" The woman laughed. "I can't believe it."

"Can't believe what?" This crazy woman continued to laugh and Kristina's puzzled confusion slowly turned to dread. Something was going on. Was this the mystery woman? Had Thomas messed up? Failed to get her to leave before she, his wife, came home?

"You were in South America? I thought it was weird, you taking off when the deal was finally closing. All those digital signatures."

"Digital signatures?"

177

The woman snorted. "I'm Carmen Dyson. I own this house. You sold it to me."

"What are you saying?" The confusion that had been building turned to dread. Thomas' quick forays out of hearing distance, rapid goodbyes, sudden departure for home. It hadn't been another woman. Well, it had. There was this woman, Carmen, but she wasn't the mystery woman.

The iPad. Digital signatures.

Thomas had sold their house.

Her husband had moved off with a newer, pliable younger woman. Taking everything.

"Sorry. Don't look so stricken. Come round, he left something for you."

Carmen didn't invite her in, just reached inside, grabbed something off the window ledge and turned back. She handed Kristina a thick white envelope. Square and plumped, like a wedding invitation ripe with return reply and directions to the reception. Then she said "I really have to go get dressed" and abruptly shut the door in Kristina's face.

Kristina slid her fingernail under the flap and opened the envelope. Had Thomas actually left her a "Dear John" letter?

There was a card, with a photo inside. She looked at the picture first.

A craftsman style home made of beautiful stone, the wide front porch a smiling mouth and the windows two shining eyes. The yard was full of blooming flowers, lending the whole thing a past era feel. She noticed the potted geranium next to the stairs.

"My dearest Kristina,

Don't take your luggage from the car. Give your driver this address: 4396 Pippen Rd. I'm waiting here for you, here in our new home.

Your loving husband, Thomas"

Her hands shook and her mouth went dry. Was this even possible? Had Thomas actually sold their house and bought a new one? She looked at the photo. The house was stunning, everything she had ever claimed to want in a home. But it just couldn't be. What kind of husband, what kind of man, no, what kind of person thought it was normal to relocate someone without even asking for their opinion on the matter?

She was frozen by the realization that her things were not here anymore. Closets of coats and sweaters, drawers filled with art supplies, kitchen cabinets with her grandmother's cast iron fry pan. Carmen's things, like those terrible olive colored curtains, had taken place of all that was hers. Kristina pulled her dried lips apart and moved her tongue around, trying to get moisture back into her mouth.

As suddenly as the air had left her body she felt her lungs fill and warmth creep back into her limbs. Her heart peeked out from behind the dark cloud, a tentative child checking to see if the coast was clear.

She pictured Thomas waiting in the new house. He had likely cooked a dinner and their blond maple table, filling a new dining room, was covered with a white linen cloth, candles waiting to be lit, wine ready to be poured. She was sure he had checked her arrival time, planned everything down to the minute, his romantic surprise burning a hole in his head as he wondered why she wasn't there yet.

She turned to the street and smiled. Waving the card, she rushed back to the car.

"You're never going to guess what happened," she said as she slipped into George's waiting arms.

The Easter Tail

(Yes, T-A-I-L)

Javier watched the mouse every day for a week. He studied the way its tiny feet scuttled across the concrete path, tail like a wire flag waving behind. He admired the effortless rise onto back haunches the mouse used to look around the garden, even though as a rabbit he too could stand up and sniff for danger. And those cheeks! Seemed like an endless amount of seeds and such could be stuffed inside, leaving the mouse looking ready for quarantine in the mumps ward.

Javier glanced down at his own thick feet. The front weren't bad, but he couldn't perform the clever tricks of the mouse. He had seen the tiny creature use those paws almost like a human. But a rabbit's hind feet? They were long and stiff, made for maximum contact with the ground in preparation for each hop. Ugly.

Then there was his tail. He had to contort, rolling onto his left hip and twisting his neck, to even glimpse the stub that sprouted out of his rump. So disappointing to be born a rabbit.

Now, if this were a story for children, our hero Javier would explore the great outdoors and be aptly jealous of the dog's tail which could wag, the cat's tail which could twitch at the tip, or the squirrel's huge fluffy flag of a tail. In the course of finding the moral to explain away his jealousy he would never notice the stub tail of the deer, or the prehistoric finger which poked out of the tortoise rump, or the fact that the frog didn't even have a tail, having re-absorbed it in the course of growing up. Somehow, through some amazing turn of events, Javier's tail would save the day and he would be content.

But this is not a story for children.

And although Javier may be a rabbit, he is not a bunny.

Well, not yet.

"You have to go to catechism," his mother insisted. "And you have to pay attention."

Why was it called catechism when no cats were allowed? Javier nibbled on his carrots, but didn't speak out loud. His mother was in a bad mood.

"Why can't Adelita be the Easter bunny?" His sister would love it, he was sure.

Mother didn't answer right away. Her ear twitched and her nose wiggled and finally she spoke. "Tradition. It is important to your father that the oldest son have the job."

Was that sarcasm he heard in his mother's voice?

Javier worked on his sister. "You'd be great at it, Adelita. Just hop around with that basket and hide all those eggs."

"We don't lay eggs."

Well, okay, maybe she was a little young to understand all

the concepts of Easter. She hadn't even started Sunday School yet, let alone Cat-a-chistics.

"It's catechism, Son. Don't be a numbskull." His father didn't get the joke.

"But don't you see? It's like gymnastics." Javier hopped up and down, waiting for his father to smile.

"Do your homework." Father's big foot zipped out and thumped Javier on the side of the head and the young rabbit slunk to his part of the warren.

Each day Javier stayed out of his father's way and continued to watch the mouse and the duck and the frog and all the other animals. As far as he could figure, no one else had to go to classes and no one else had to worry about doing a job which made no sense.

"Mother, why isn't there an Easter duck?"

"Why isn't there an Easter frog?"

"Mother, people eat eggs all the time, why do they want more on Easter?"

When his mother refused to answer any more questions—she no longer would even nod and pretend—he asked his teacher.

"You shouldn't question the word of our Lord."

What kind of answer was that? Javier pulled his long ears tight to the back of his head and thumped the dirt with his hind foot. Of course, this was not an acceptable response to a teacher and he was sent outside.

Ah…outside. Where he could resume his study of his fellow forest friends. Except he was told to come back in after five minutes time out, so he didn't dare explore the wide, wonderful world.

Now, if this were a story for teenagers, Javier would discover something—oh, say magic—or he would sharpen his teeth and turn into a vampire rabbit or he would at least don a cape and fly out to rescue someone. Probably his younger sister, and it would all come together somehow to make him happy that he was the one picked to deliver the eggs.

This is not a story for teenagers.

"And those of you chosen to spread the word of our Lord by delivering colored eggs must understand this message." Master Rabbit paced back and forth in front of the chosen bunnies. Thirty young rabbits who would carry on the long, long tradition of delivering baskets full of eggs.

Javier felt his head droop and his eyes close. The master's voice sounded like the soft drone of a bumblebee. What if he had wings? Could he fly away and never come back? Where would he fly? Was there a place in this world were rabbits were free from Easter?

The next day Javier kissed Mother goodbye, tugged on Adelita's ear, and hopped off to school. Only he didn't go to school. He didn't start out with the idea that he would play hooky, but that mouse was running down the path like there was something exciting and Javier couldn't help but follow. Of course, it turned out the mouse wasn't really going anywhere important but by that time a butterfly had caught the truant rabbit's attention and then there was a mockingbird and a turkey vulture and three crickets and…well any of you who have ever suffered distractions get it. Javier never made it to school that day.

But he was no dumb bunny. Javier made sure to go home at three o'clock, hoping he had some small chance of not being caught for his deception.

"How in the world did you get so dirty?" Mother's nose twitched double time. "What's that smell?"

He glanced down at his brown fur. Grass stains, pine tar, river mud, and some sort of yellow pollen. "Uh...I fell?"

Just then Father walked in. One only had to look at his wild-eyed face to know Javier was not going to escape punishment this time around.

Now if this were a story for adults Javier would be abused, and maybe even Mother and Adelita would be abused, or perhaps his father would attempt to abuse them and Javier would stand up for them, or maybe even feel guilty because he didn't stand up for them and they would escape or not escape. In any case, there would be a lot of emotion and tension and plot development and such.

This is not a story for adults.

So Javier took his thumping and promised never to cut school again and slunk off cursing under his breath that his father was an asshole and he would be sorry. He spent the next day ignoring the lecture on the resurrection and thinking about humans and rabbits and tails. And during lunch break he never even looked back as he hopped away from the meadow where classes were held.

Once out of sight he turned up the speed. The young rabbit raced down the trail as if a fox were hot on his tail. He twisted and dodged and leapt and never slowed for an instant, even when his chest burned and his feet stung.

Javier ran all the way to the edge of the forest and finally stopped when he could see the town. Panting and licking his dry lips, wishing for some water, he stared at the buildings. It didn't take him long to spot the church with the spire and the bell tower. He kept to the edge of the road, using the tall grass as cover.

It was easy to slip inside, as the door was propped open with a rock. Javier hopped softly under the bench, sniffing the shoes and legs that formed a wall between him and whatever was at the front of the church. He stopped and adjusted his ears, tilting the right towards the front of the room and swiveling the left to catch any sounds from behind.

"And the Lord said…"

Yep, just like his teacher said. Humans went to school too, and all these people were listening to a lecture.

"And so Christ died for our sins according to the Scriptures, he was buried, he rose again on the third day according to the Scriptures, and he appeared to Peter and then to the Twelve."

Hmmm…nothing about rabbits. Or eggs for that matter.

Javier listened and listened. Finally the deep voice stopped and another, higher pitched voice took over.

"We only have a few announcements today. The coat drive is over next Friday and we would still like twenty more coats to take to the shelter, so check those closets. Any children who want to participate in the delivery are welcome, call Nancy Penji and let her know. The Easter party will be on Saturday at eleven o'clock. Remember, Easter eggs and rabbits are pagan rituals and we encourage you to come to the party for a true celebration and forgo the tradition which has nothing to do with being a real Christian."

What? Javier wished for a rewind button, but he was absolutely sure she had just said bunnies and eggs were out. He waited a few minutes to see if there would be more, but she was finished and everyone was standing and he dashed out the door to escape discovery.

He almost made it out unseen, but as Javier raced down the steps he heard a voice.

"Mommy! I just saw the Easter Bunny."

"Hush, that was just a rabbit. There is no such thing as the Easter Bunny."

"And then they said 'There's no such thing as the Easter Bunny.'" Javier tried to keep very still while reporting to his mother. It was hard to keep from hopping up and down with excitement, but he knew she wouldn't listen if he acted like a foolish kit.

"You went to town? Haven't you been told NEVER to go there?" Mother glanced over her shoulder. "You promised your father you would not cut school."

"But Mother, don't you see? I don't need to go to school. What they're teaching is a lie. We aren't even supposed to deliver eggs, it's a...paper, no that's not right, PAGAN, that's it.

It's a pagan ritual." Javier realized he didn't really know what that meant, but maybe Mother did. Why wouldn't she just listen?

"It is our tradition, Javier. It's important to your father. Can't you just leave well enough alone and do it? One day a year, that's all I'm asking." Her whiskers quivered.

Javier didn't give up. He tried to explain to his mother how silly it was to be something they were not. He tried to tell her that she had been blindly following something that made no sense. He tried to convince her that times change and the old ways may have been fine at one time, but new things were good too. He tried and tried, day after day. He was extra helpful, he threw a tantrum. He offered to take Adelita and her friends to the meadow and watch while they played.

Mother wouldn't listen. And if she wouldn't listen what chance did he have of convincing his father? Javier felt the ache of yesterday's thumping on his hip. The only thing he would get from Father was a bruise on the other side to match this one.

So Javier put on his cape—okay, not really, but this little kit was destined to be a hero—and went out to find the other young rabbits. If the old ones wouldn't listen, maybe the next generation would.

And the next generation did. And no rabbit ever delivered eggs again.

So you see dear reader, this story is for rabbits. Rabbits like young Javier who were prisoners to tradition and forced—make that enslaved—into delivering colored eggs year after year when nothing about the whole process has anything to do with being a rabbit. But there was a revolution and it worked and that is why you, dear reader, spend the night before Easter hiding eggs for your young and telling them the lie that has been perpetuated by rabbits stuck on tradition.

"Let's go see what the Easter Bunny left for you."

ABOUT THE AUTHOR

Robin Martinez Rice is a retired Educational Psychologist and Marriage Family Therapist taking advantage of the time off. Traveling in her old time RV—"The Bookmobile"—she writes in in National Parks, next to rivers and with a view of the ocean.

Author of

Imperfecta

Sisters in Pieces

Tales of the Elemental Goddesses

Hidden Within the Stones

Visit her Amazon author page or her website at www.robinmartinezrice.com for more information.

Credits

"Day-of-the-Not-So-Dead" appeared in *The Walrus*, Mills College Literary Journal, 2014

"Separate Vacations" appeared in the anthology *Holidazed*, 2016

www.ingramcontent.com/pod-product-compliance
Lightning Source LLC
Chambersburg PA
CBHW061157170626
46809CB00003B/1141